HOW THE HEDGEHOG MARRIED
AND OTHER CROATIAN FAIRY TALES

KAKO SE JE JEŽ OŽENIO
I DRUGE HRVATSKE NARODNE BAJKE

HOW THE HEDGEHOG MARRIED
AND OTHER CROATIAN FAIRY TALES

KAKO SE JE JEŽ OŽENIO
I DRUGE HRVATSKE NARODNE BAJKE

SELECTED AND TRANSLATED BY
DASHA C. NISULA

COVER AND INTERIOR ILLUSTRATIONS BY
JOSIP BOTTERI DINI

singular fiction, poetry, nonfiction, translation, drama, and graphic books

Library and Archives Canada Cataloguing in Publication

Title: How the hedgehog married : and other Croatian fairy tales = Kako se je jež oženio : I druge hrvatske narodne bajke / selected and translated by Dasha C. Nisula ; cover and illustrations by Josip Botteri Dini.
Other titles: Kako se je jež oženio | container of (work): Kako se je jež oženio (Nisula) | container of (expression): Kako se je jež oženio (Nisula). English
Names: Nisula, Dasha Culic, editor, translator. | Botteri Dini, Josip, 1943- illustrator.
Identifiers: Canadiana 20210315792 | ISBN 9781550969658 (softcover)
Subjects: LCSH: Fairy tales—Croatia. | LCSH: Fairy tales—Croatia—Translations into English.
Classification: LCC GR254 .K3513 2022 | DDC 398.2094972—dc23

Translation copyright © Dasha C. Nisula, 2022
Book designed by Michael Callaghan
Typeset in Times New Roman, UnZialish, Bill Clarke Caps, Zapfino (with instances of Bembo, Granjon, King Arthur, University Old Style, and Vecna) fonts at Moons of Jupiter Studios
Published by Exile Editions Ltd. www.ExileEditions.com
144483 Southgate Road 14—GD, Holstein, Ontario, N0G 2A0
Printed and Bound in Canada by Marquis Book Printing

Canadian sales representation: The Canadian Manda Group,
664 Annette Street, Toronto ON M6S 2C8.
www.mandagroup.com 416 516 0911.

North American and international distribution, and U.S. sales:
Independent Publishers Group, 814 North Franklin Street,
Chicago IL 60610 www.ipgbook.com toll free: 1 800 888 4741.

for all the children
young and old
who never had a chance
to read fairy tales
from this part of the world

Introduction

For decades now there has been a growing interest in fairy tales, appearing in print, adaptations to opera, ballet, theater, film, design, art, animated cartoons, and in toys and games that are part of our daily life. Once delegated to grandparents to read at bedtime, or, even earlier, told or read to adult audiences for entertainment, fairy tales today have attracted adults who view them with as much interest as the children. No doubt, current technological advances and magnificent visual reproductions have further propelled the interest of both young and old audiences, and what has happened in the process is that the old tale structure has been artistically expanded to offer us glimpses into multiple variations of that once simple skeleton of a tale. Artistic tales are more flexible and are considered to have a more open form and embellished language. Transformations of old structures still delight, entertain, and enlighten the public. Fairy tales have not lost their audience, but today, dressed in contemporary technologically colorful outfits, they have been transformed to perform assignments and face challenges in the language of the 21st century. It need not worry us if these artistically suggestive images of well-known fairy tale characters present new pictures in our mind's eye; after all, we will always have the basic original sketch of the preserved oral tradition of ancient fairy tales to read and allow our own imagination to be creative. One may even develop a desire to see how a particular character in a tale has been transformed over a period of time.

However, it is on the basis of the national tale, with a strong structure and content, that tales we now call artistic or literary actually developed. We know that the core structure of the national tale is strong and does not deviate – it includes the fantastical beginning, the middle part in which a hero and/or a heroine are challenged, and the triumphant end. Magic is at the center in a fairy tale where two worlds meet, the real and the fantastic. In such a situation, anything becomes possible: a frog transforms into a maiden, a hedgehog into

a young man, a snake into a prince, a groom, a maiden, and a rosemary bush just might turn into a living beauty. Another characteristic of a fairy tale is the fact that it does not disclose a particular place or time, or, where and when the action in the fairy tale takes place. Events are beyond the seven seas, many mountains, or some thrice-nine kingdom, a very long time ago. But what does happen in fairy tales is quite similar in that either a young man or a maiden venture out into the world where they will be tested. The strength of the thematic formula in a fairy tale concerns some assignment, challenge, or conflict that the main character must experience and resolve, and it is then that the magic appears and solves the initial conflict. Attempts to resolve the problem or complete the task repeat in threes until the resolution is achieved. Only then does the tale formula bring the character home. Not all fairy tales, of course, have a happy ending, and there are always some deviations in the existing structure.

Tales have existed as long as man from the beginning of time as part of the living oral tradition. However, written fairy tales came about later in relation to the oral tradition. Macleod Yearsley called them "fiction in its earliest stages." The first person to compile a collection of fairy tales, and the first known printed version of fairy tales in Europe, is by the Venetian writer Giovanni Francesco Straparola, with his *Le Piacevoli Notti* (*The Pleasant Nights)* printed in 1551. And the first national collection of fairy tales is considered to be *Il Pentamerone* (*The Tale of Tales*), attributed to Giambattista Basile of Naples, Italy, published in early 17th century, 1634-1636. In the late 17th century, we have Charles Perrault, a French author who laid the foundation for a new literary genre, the fairy tale. His collection of tales, *Histoires ou contes du temps passé* (*Stories or Fairy Tales from Past Times*), published in 1697, was based on French popular traditions and it influenced the Brothers Grimm, Wilhelm and Jacob. Then in the early 18th century, the first European version of *Arabian Nights* in French, translated by Antoine Galland, was published in 1704-1717. An anonymous English version of *Arabian Nights*, titled *The Arabian Nights' Entertainments*, became the first English-language edition in 1706. About a hundred years later, by the time

of Romanticism in the early 19th century, when interest in folklore in general was on the rise, a collection of German tales by the Brothers Grimm, *Kinder- und Hausmärchen (Children's and Household Tales),* came out in print in 1812. The Brothers Grimm's last modified edition came out in 1857. Still, another collection of literary tales was written by a Danish writer, Hans Christian Andersen, whose first fairy tales were published in 1835, followed by *Fairy Tales Told for Children* in 1838.

One of the largest collections in the world is that by Alexander Afanasyev, who in the mid-1850s published his first edition of *Narodniye russkiye skazki (Russian Fairy Tales)*. Between 1855 and 1867 he compiled some 600 folk tales and fairy tales and is known as the Russian counterpart to the Brothers Grimm. His collection had influence on the works of many Russian writers and composers. There is yet another counterpart to the Brothers Grimm, a Croatian writer of the early 20th century, Ivana Brlić-Mažuranić, who in 1916 published in Zagreb her collection titled *Priče iz davnine (Croatian Tales of Long Ago)*.

Croatian fairy tales have a long tradition and belong to the Slavic folklore belt, which extends from the most western edge of the Adriatic Sea, eastward over the Danube Valley and Carpathian Mountains, all the way to the Ural Mountains. They differ from the fairy tales of the East Slavic group in that Russian, Ukrainian, and Belorussian fairy tales held on longer to the ancient mythological Slavic motifs. If we keep in mind that Christian beliefs and practices rest upon the rich ancient Slavic myths and beliefs, there are still remnants of that ancient Slavic tradition in the fairy tales. Ancient Slavs worshiped nature, Perun, the god of thunder, Mokosh, the goddess of earth, water and the wind, the sun, moon and stars, trees and animals. No wonder one can encounter these in the tales and recognize remnants of their good and bad traits.

The more westward the tales are, the fewer Slavic mythological associations appear in them, and in looking at Russian tales, for example, Slavic mythological images are more apparent than in Croatian tales. Yet the similarities not only between the Slavic tales but tales in general are

overwhelming – the life force of a fairy tale depends upon the similarities to and differences from the tales in their proximity. As for the Croatian tales, they are in a territory near Straparola's, Perrault's, as well as the Brothers Grimm's and Andersen's tales. But what is of interest in Ivana Brlić-Mažuranić's collection is precisely the similarities to and differences from these well-known collections which are readily available in English translation. However, there is not much available in English of the Croatian tales. In fact, only one book exists in English, translated by Fanny S. Copeland and published in 1922 under the title *Croatian Tales of Long Ago*.

My selection of tales is based on the material I translated and used in my courses on Slavic mythology which I taught for over a decade at Western Michigan University. These classes were popular and moved me to include among the well-known Slavic fairy tales some Croatian ones which are less known and essentially unavailable in English until now. I anticipate that this selection of Croatian fairy tales in translation will be of interest to readers in general, and to those engaged in a more comparative and analytical approach to fairy tales. The focus in this volume has been on preserving the elemental structure of the oral tradition without embellishment, meaning that the tales in this book are as pure as we can get them and closest to their original oral tradition we have in Croatian literature.

Many Croatian fairy tales do not end tragically, but often the good triumphs over evil and characters who are noble and innocent beings find themselves in the world of magic and ultimately succeed. Goodness, honesty, integrity, and fidelity always win in the end. If we look closely, this means that fairy tales ultimately have some instructional purpose for the young while entertaining the community. In addition, if one focuses on the awkwardness of fairy tale heroes or heroines, we can also deduce that the focus of the fairy tale is usually on the difficult transitional stages of growing up and growing old, essentially life struggles which we may experience vicariously while reading the fairy tale itself.

—D. C. N.

Once upon a time,
a long time ago,
far beyond the Seven Seas,
there lived ...

... then there was a wedding,
and I was there.

About Lizard The Bridegroom

O Gušteru Mladoženji

O GUŠTERU MLADOŽENJI

*T*ako su dugo vremena zajedno živjeli muž i žena i nisu djece imali. Uvijek su Boga molili da bi im dao bar jedno dijete, pa makar to dijete bilo maleno kao gušter. Ovaj je put dragi Bog uslišao njihovu molbu i dao im je dijete, ali dijete je bilo gušter. Otac i majka voljeli su toga guštera kao pravo svoje dijete. Gušter je pomalo rastao i napredovao. Tako je dorastao do šesnaeste godine i onda rekao materi da bi se rado oženio i neka ide otac za njega isprositi kraljevu kćer.

Otac se je tome protivio na sve načine, sam nije mogao razumjeti kako bi to mogao učiniti. Ali kad mu sin gušter nije dao nikako mira, išao je kralju. Kralj je saslušao oca i rekao mu da će on dati svoju kćer njegovu sinu za ženu ako njegov sin dokotura po cesti jaje, od svoje kuće do njegova kraljevskoga dvora, a da se jaje ne polupa.

Uzeo je gušter jaje kad mu je otac rekao što kralj ište od njega i dokoturao je jaje od svoje kuće do kraljevskoga dvora a da jaje nije puklo. Sad je išao gušter sam kralju i tražio od njega njegovu kćer za ženu. Ali kralj mu nije dao kćeri, nego mu je rekao da će dobiti njegovu kćer za ženu tek onda kada bude imao ljepše konje i ljepšu kočiju nego li on, kralj. Taj je gušter išao odmah tražiti po cijelom svijetu najljepše konje i najljepšu kočiju, dok nije našao ljepše konje i ljepšu kočiju nego li je imao kralj.

Došao je opet pred kralja i stade opet tražiti od njega kćer za ženu. Ali kralj mu nije dao ni sada svoje kćeri, nego mu je rekao da će dobiti njegovu kćer za ženu tek onda kada bude imao ljepši dvorac nego li kralj. Gušter je počeo odmah graditi dvorac, gradio ga tri godine, a kad ga je sagradio bio je

ABOUT LIZARD
THE BRIDEGROOM

*A*n old man and his wife lived together for a long time, but they had no children. They always prayed that God would give them at least one child, even if that child would be as small as a lizard. One day God heard their prayer and gave them a child, but the child was born a lizard. The father and mother loved that lizard as their real child. The lizard thrived. He grew up to be sixteen years of age and then said to his mother that he would like to get married. He wanted his father to go and ask for the hand of the king's daughter in marriage.

The father did his best to oppose this request; he could not figure out how to go about it. But as the lizard son would give him no peace, the father went to the king. The king listened to the father and agreed to give his daughter as a wife under one condition. The son would have to roll an egg down the street from his house to the king's palace without breaking it.

The lizard took an egg as the king had ordered, and he rolled it from his house to the king's palace without breaking it. Then the lizard went himself to the king and asked for the king's daughter to be his wife. The king did not give him his daughter, but told him that he may have her as his wife only when he has better horses and a more elegant carriage than the king has. Immediately, the lizard went to seek the most beautiful horses and the most beautiful carriage in the world, and he eventually found more beautiful horses and a more beautiful carriage than what the king had.

Again he came before the king and began to ask for the king's daughter to be his wife. But the king still would not give him his daughter and told him

njegov dvorac ljepši nego li kraljev. Sada je išao opet gušter pred kralja i tražio je od njega da mu dade svoju kćer za ženu, jer da je sve učinio što je od njega tražio. I kralj mu je sada morao dati kćer za ženu. I tako su se vjenčali kraljeva kći i gušter.

Kraljeva je kći uvijek plakala jer je uzela za muža guštera, a kad ga je već morala uzeti nastojala je da ga se što prije riješi. Jednom dođe k njoj neka starica i upita je zašto uvijek plače. Ona joj otkrije svu svoju tugu i žalost. Starica njoj na to kaže: "Ništa ti ne plači, već ti pripazi kad se tvoj muž u večer svuče iz one kože, pa gledaj da vatru u peći dobro zakuriš i onda baci njegovu kožu u vatru. Ti ćeš vidjeti, kako je on lijep čovjek, kad nema one kože!" Kraljeva je kći onako učinila kako ju je starica nagovorila i u jutro vidjela da joj je muž bez one kože lijep, da ljepšega nije bilo na cijelom ovom svijetu.

Kad se on u jutro digao, tražio je svoju kožu da će se u nju obući ali je nije mogao naći i kad se je uvjerio da je nema nigdje, rekao je ženi: "Ja znam, da si ti to meni učinila i da je tvojom krivnjom nestalo moje kože. Sad ja odlazim, a ti se ne rastala s onim, što pod srcem nosiš (bila je trudna), dok ne metnem na tebe svoju desnu ruku!" i otišao je.

Deset je godina ona dijete nosila i nije se mogla s njime rastati. Kad je vidjela da se drukčije ne će moći riješiti djeteta, išla je muža po svijetu tražiti. Tako je došla do Vjetra i pitala ga je za svoga muža, da li znade gdje je. On je rekao da ne zna, ali da će pitati svoga oca, možda će on za nj znati. Pitaju oni staroga Vjetra, ali ni on nije znao gdje je. Stari je Vjetar uputi da ide k Jugu, a za uspomenu joj je dao Vjetar zlatni stolac. Došla je ona do Juga i pitala za svoga muža. I on joj reče da ne zna gdje je i nagovori je da ide do Bure, jer da Bura svaki kut potraži, a za uspomenu joj je dao zlatnu preslicu i zlatnu kudjelju.

Došla je ona do Bure i upita i nju za svoga muža. Bura nije u prvi čas znala, ali je odmah zapuhnula i tražila ga po svima i najdaljim stranama, dok ga nije našla. Kad ga je našla, dala je toj kraljevoj kćeri jednu kvočku s pilićima, pa joj je rekla: "Ajde, nije daleko, doći ćeš do takve i takve kuće i

that he may have the daughter only when he has a more beautiful castle than the king's. The lizard began to build a castle at once, and he continued to build it for three years. When he had finished, he had a castle more beautiful than the king's. Once more the lizard went to the king and asked to marry his daughter because he had done everything the king had asked him to do. Now the king had to give him his daughter as a wife. And so the king's daughter and the lizard were married.

The king's daughter had been crying all the time because she would have to take a lizard as her husband, and once they were married she tried to get rid of him as soon as she could. One day an old woman came to her and asked why she was always crying. The daughter revealed to the old woman her distress and sorrow. The old woman then said: "Do not cry, but at night when your lizard husband removes his skin, see to it that the fire is stoked. Then throw his skin into the stove. You will see what a handsome man he is when he doesn't have that skin!" The king's daughter did as the old woman told her, and in the morning she saw that her husband was handsome without the skin, and there was no one more handsome in this whole world.

When her husband got up in the morning, he looked for his skin to put it on, but he could not find it. Once he was sure it was gone, he said to his wife: "I know that you did this to me and that you are responsible for my missing skin. I will leave now, but do not separate yourself from the one you carry under your heart until I put my right hand upon you!" And he left knowing she was with child.

For ten years she carried the child and could not separate herself from it. When she realized that there could be no other way to separate from the child, she went in search of her husband throughout the world. She came to the Wind and asked about her husband, whether the Wind might know where he was. The Wind said he didn't know, but would ask his father, Old Wind, who might know. The Old Wind didn't know either. He sent her to the South Wind, and gave her a golden stool as a remembrance. So she came to the South Wind and asked about her husband. The South Wind also told her

u toj je kući tvoj muž sa jednom drugom mladom ženskom. Pred tom kućom raspusti tvoje piliće i kvočku, pa sjedni na svoj zlatni stolac i predi na svojoj zlatnoj preslici svoju zlatnu kudjelju. Kad te vidi izaći će ona žena, pa će te pitati da li ćeš prodati svoju zlatnu preslicu i zlatnu kudjelju. Ti reci, da ne ćeš prodati, nego da ćeš joj dati ako te pusti jednu noć kraj svoga muža spavati. Ona će na to pristati, a ti mu reci, kad ćeš kraj njega leći: Zvjezdani kralju, zvjezdani kralju, baci na me desnu ruku svoju, da ti čedo rodim! On će baciti na te svoju desnu ruku i ti ćeš odmah njemu poroditi sina i riješit ćeš se bremena što ga već deset godina nosiš!”

Otiđe kraljeva kći dalje i dođe do one kuće, sjede na svoj zlatni stolac, raspusti svoju kvočku i piliće i stade presti na zlatnoj preslici zlatnu kudjelju. Opazi je žena iz kuće i upita je bi li prodala svoju preslicu i kudjelju. Kraljeva joj kći odgovori: “Ne ću draga, prodati, nego ću ti dati, ako me pustiš jednu noć spavati kraj tvoga muža!” Ta je žena na to pristala i uzela odmah zlatnu preslicu i zlatnu kudjelju.

Uvečer je dala žena svome mužu nekakav teški napitak i on je odmah teško usnuo i ništa nije čuo o čemu je prva žena govorila. Ujutro pođe opet kaljeva kći pred kuću, sjede na svoj zlatni stolac i raspusti svoje piliće i kvočku. Izađe opet ta žena iz kuće i upita je opet da li će prodati svoju kvočku i piliće. Kraljeva joj kći govori: “Ne ću, draga, prodati, nego ću ti dati, ako me pustiš još jednu noć spavati kraj tvoga muža!” Ova je ženska opet pristala na to i uzela odmah kvočku i piliće.

Uvečer je dala ova žena opet svomu mužu neki teški napitak i on je odmah teško usnuo i nije opet ništa čuo, što mu je ta prava njegova žena govorila. Sad je vidjela Bura, da ne će ta mlada žena sama ništa napraviti, stoga je došla ona sama k tomu mladomu čovjeku, a izgledala kao neka starica, i rekla mu: “Nemoj večeras ništa piti što će ti dati tvoja žena, nego baci što ti dade u kraj da ona ne opazi. Vidjet ćeš nešto i ne će ti biti žao!” Opet izađe u jutro kraljeva kći pred kuću i sjede na svoj zlatni stolac. Dođe za njom iz kuće i ona žena i upita je opet da li će prodati svoj zlatni stolac. Kraljeva joj kći odgovori: “Ne ću, draga, prodati, nego ću ti dati ako me pustiš još jednu noć

he didn't know and sent her to Bura, the North-East Wind who knows every corner of the world. As a remembrance he gave her a golden distaff and golden hemp.

When she came to Bura, she asked about her husband. Bura did not know at once, but immediately blew and sought him in the farthest corners until the husband was located. Bura did find him, and gave the king's daughter a hen with chicks and said: "Go, it's not far. You'll come to a house, and in that house you'll find your husband with another young woman. In front of that house release your chicks, then sit on your golden stool, and spin golden hemp on your golden distaff. When she sees you, the woman will come out and ask if you would sell her your golden distaff and golden hemp. You say that you will not, but that you will give them to her if she lets you sleep near her husband for one night. She will agree to that, and when you sleep next to him tell him, 'Star-lit King, Star-lit King, put your right hand upon me, so I can give birth to your child!' He'll put upon you his right arm, and you'll immediately bear him a son and be rid of your ten-year pregnancy!"

The king's daughter continued on her way and came to the house, sat on her golden stool, released her hen and chicks, and began to spin on her golden distaff the golden hemp. The woman in the house noticed her and asked if she would sell the distaff and hemp. The king's daughter said: "I will not sell them, dear, but I will give them to you if you let me sleep one night near your husband!" The woman agreed to that and immediately took the golden distaff and golden hemp.

That evening the woman gave her husband a strong drink, and he immediately fell into a deep sleep and heard nothing that his first wife said. In the morning again the king's daughter went in front of the house, sat on her golden stool and released her hen and chicks. The woman again came out from the house and asked her if she would sell her hen and chicks. The king's daughter again replied: "I will not sell them, dear, but I will give them to you if you will let me sleep one night more near your husband!" The woman again agreed and immediately took the hen and chicks.

spavati kraj tvoga muža!" Ta je žena opet pristala na to i uzela odmah zlatni stolac.

Uvečer je dala ova žena opet svome mužu nekakav teški napitak, ali ga on nije ovaj put popio nego ga je bacio u kraj a da ona nije opazila. Kada je kraljeva kći legla do njega i rekla mu: "Zvjezdani kralju, zvjezdani kralju, baci na me desnu ruku svoju da ti čedo rodim!" odmah se je on k njoj okrenuo, bacio na nju svoju desnu ruku i ona je odmah sina porodila. Sada ju je istom muž prepoznao. Odmah su se spremili i drugi dan u zoru zajedno sa djetetom svojim vratili u svoju domovinu.

Kralj je bio vrlo veseo što su mu se djeca sretno vratila i što je imao tako lijepoga zeta. Od velika veselja priredio je veliku gozbu i pozvao u goste silu naroda iz svoje kraljevine. I ja sam bila tam, jela i pila, pripovijest je van!

In the evening the woman again gave her husband another strong drink, and he immediately fell into a deep sleep and again heard nothing the real wife was saying. Bura now realized that the young woman alone could not accomplish anything and appeared to the young man in the form of an old woman, saying: "Don't drink anything your wife gives you tonight, but throw it out on the side so she doesn't see it. You will see something, and you won't be sorry!" In the morning the king's daughter again came out of the house and took her seat on the golden stool. The woman also came out after her and asked if the king's daughter would sell her golden stool. The king's daughter answered: "I will not sell it, dear, but I'll give it to you if you let me sleep near your husband one night more!" The woman agreed again and at once took the golden stool.

In the evening the woman again gave her husband a strong drink, and this time he did not drink it, but he threw it out to the side so the woman would not notice. When the king's daughter lay next to him, she said: "Star-lit King, Star-lit King, put your right hand upon me, so I can give birth to your child!" He turned toward her, put his right arm upon her, and she immediately bore him a son. At that moment he recognized her. The next day at dawn they returned to their homeland with the child.

The king was very happy they had returned safely, and he had such a handsome son-in-law. With great joy he arranged for a party and invited many people from his kingdom to his palace. And I was there; I ate and I drank. The tale has been told!

Fairy's Blood Brother

Vilin Pobratim

VILIN POBRATIM

*B*io kralj. Imao kćer lijepu i prelijepu. Svako se je čudom čudio njezinoj ljepoti. Prose je kraljevići i gospoda, ali ona neće da se uda. Otac kralj kaže: "Udaćeš se za junaka. Čuo sam, ima tamo negdje na svijetu kralj, u koga ima ptica, što nese zlatna jaja. Pticu čuvaju u zlatnom kavezu u kraljevu vrtu, zidom ograđenu, da ne može ni ptica zida preletjeti, tako je visok. Na vratima stražu straže dva lava, i dva risa, i dva mrka vuka, i dva slona trbonoše, i dva hrta brzonoga. Ko hoće oženiti se mojom kćerju, mora mi dobaviti onu pticu što nese zlatna jaja, i donijeti je s kavezom iz kraljeva vrta, bilo milom bilo silom."

Bio jedan momak. Vidi ljepotu djevoju, kraljevu kćerku. Omiljela mu, i on njoj. Momak vene i sahne u čami dan i noć; niti jede, niti pije, samo misli za djevojkom. I djevojku zanose misli za momkom, ali otac kralj ostane pri svom. Momak ide po lovu, da se malo rastrese i razbije srcu jade. U šumi nađe u jednom šipragu guju uprocijepljenu. Frućka se i čiči. Ne može se izvući iz procijepa. Momak bliže pristupi. Guja ga moli: "Da si mi po bogu brat, junače! Izbavi me iz procijepa, biću ti od pomoći." Momak se smiluje i oslobodi guju, a ona mu reče: "Idem s tobom; nemoj se ništa bojati, nego me pazi kao sestru, a ja ću tebe kao brata." Tako i bude.

Ode momak iz šume doma. Guja otplazi za njim te mu reče: "Sakriću se u tvojoj kući, a kad ideš spavati u tvoju ložnicu, vidjećemo se tamo. Onda mi možeš kazati, u čemu ti ja mogu biti od pomoći!" Kad uveče dođe momak u svoju ložnicu spavati, guja izlazi ispod postelje i kaže: "Ne boj se; ja ću svući sad sa sebe gujsku košulju; vidjećeš ko sam."

Guja svuče sa sebe gujsku košuljicu i pretvori se u bijelu vilu. Momak se začudi, a vila mu kaže: "Junače, pobratime, kaži mi slobodno od kakve ti

FAIRY'S BLOOD BROTHER

*T*here once lived a king who had a beautiful, more than beautiful daughter. Everyone was amazed by her beauty. Princes and noblemen asked for her hand, but she did not want to wed. Her father, the king, said: "You will marry a hero. I hear that there is a king somewhere in the world who has a bird that lays golden eggs. The bird is kept in a golden cage in the king's garden, which is surrounded by a wall that is so high that even a bird cannot fly over it. The gates are guarded by two lions, two lynx, two stern wolves, two big-bellied elephants, and two fast-legged greyhounds. Whoever wants to marry my daughter must bring to me, either willingly or by force, the bird from the king's garden that lays golden eggs in a cage."

One day a young man saw the beauty, the king's daughter. He liked her and she liked him. The young man began to waste away and was pining away day and night. He neither ate nor drank, and he only thought about the maiden. She too only had thoughts of him, but her father, the king, remained unrelenting. The young man went hunting to distract himself and relieve his heartache. In the forest he found a viper stuck in a thicket. It hissed and squealed. It could not free itself from the thicket. The youth approached, and the viper begged him: "Be a brother to me, by God, hero! Free me from the thicket; I'll be of help to you." The young man was merciful and freed the viper, and she said to him: "I am going with you; don't be afraid, but watch me as your own sister, and I will watch you as my brother." And so it was.

He then went home from the forest. The viper crept along behind him and said: "I will hide in your house, and when you go to sleep in your room, we will see each other there. Then you can tell me how I may be of help to

15

mogu biti pomoći!" Momak odmah kaže vili posestrimi svoje jade, kako se je zagledao u ljepotu djevojku, kraljevu kćer, i ona bi rado za njega pošla, ali otac kralj traži, da mu junak zet donese pticu, štono tamo negdje u svijetu kralju, svome gospodaru, nese zlatna jaja. "Junače pobratime," veli ona, "ne znam ni ja u kog je to kralja na svijetu ptica, što nese zlatna jaja. Vodiću te sjutra Vjetrovoj majci i molićemo je, naka pita svog sina Vjetra, gdje je taj kralj i ta ptica na svijetu. Vjetar ide svuda po svijetu. Možebit on zna za tu pticu."

Kad pred zoru, momak se probudi, a vila je obukla svoju gujsku košulju, te se opet pretvorila u guju. Tada reče momku: "Nosi me u svojoj torbi, pokazaću ti put k Vjetrovoj majci." Tako i bude. Kad dođu k Vjetrovoj majci, zamole je, neka pita svoga sina za pticu, što nese zlatna jaja. Vjetrova majka sakrije momka u svom domu, da ga vjetar ne raznese, kad dođe doma na večeru. "Vjetar je, moj sinko," veli Vjetrova majka, "kadšto zle volje."

No onu večer dođe Vjetar tih i miran. Majka mu kaže za goste. Vjetar je dobre volje, zovne goste na večeru. Gosti mu kažu što su i kako su došli. Vjetar smišlja i razmišlja, pak veli: "Ja nijesam nigdje na svijetu vidio takve ptice. No ako sam možebit i vidio, nijesam zavirio u gnijezdo ptičje, pa ne znam; nego idite vi Mjesečevoj majci, neka ona pita svoga sina Mjeseca; on po noći mjesečinom zaviruje u svaku luknju i pukotinu, kroz svaki žlijeb i prozor. Možebit je on gdjegod vidio takovu pticu."

Putnici su prenoćili kod Vjetrove majke, pak sjutradan put pod noge odu tražiti Mjesečevu majku. Kad dođu k njoj, ona ih lijepo primi na konak. Morali su dugo čekati, dok je Mjesec pun došao doma k majci svojoj na večeru. Za večerom kažu gosti, što su došli. Mjesec smišlja i razmišlja, pa kaže: "Ja nijesam nigdje vidio takve ptice; barem se ne sjećam. Nego znate što: idite vi k Sunčevoj majci. Možebit je Sunce gdjegod vidjelo tu pticu."

Sjutradan odu junak i njegova posestrima vila opet na put k Sunčevoj majci. I tamo prispiju oko zapada sunca. Sunčeva majka primi goste na konak, ali ih sakrije u ledenicu, da ih Sunce ne bi spalilo i spržilo. Kad dođe Sunce svojoj majci na večeru, kaže mu majka, što je i kako je; je li vidjelo Sunce

you!" When in the evening the young man came to his room to sleep, the viper appeared from under the bed and said: "Don't be afraid; I'll take off my viper skin, and now you will see who I am." The viper removed her viper skin and turned into a white fairy. The young man was surprised, and the fairy said to him: "Hero, be my blood brother and tell me freely how I may be of help to you!" The young man immediately told the fairy, as to a sister, of his sorrow; he had seen a beautiful maiden, who would gladly marry him. However, her father, the king, had demanded that any suitor must be a hero and bring from some other kingdom in the world a bird that lays golden eggs for her master. "Hero, my brother," she said, "I don't know either where there is a king who has a bird that lays golden eggs. In the morning I will take you to the Wind's mother and request that she ask her son the Wind where in the world there is such a king and such a bird. The Wind goes everywhere in the world and perhaps knows of such a bird."

Just before dawn, the young man awoke finding that the fairy had already put on her viper skin and had turned back into a viper. She said to the young man: "Carry me in your bag, and I will show you the way to the Wind's mother." So it was. When they arrived at the home of the Wind's mother, they asked her to talk to her son about the bird that lays golden eggs. The Wind's mother hid the young man in her home, so the Wind wouldn't blow him away when he arrived home for supper. "My son, the Wind," said the Wind's mother, "is sometimes in a bad mood."

But that night the Wind was silent and calm. The mother told him about the guests. Because the Wind was in a good mood, she called the guests to supper. The guests told the Wind who they were and why they had come. The Wind thought and thought, and then said: "I have not seen such a bird anywhere in the world. But even if I had seen it, I would not have peeked into its nest and wouldn't know if the eggs were golden. But you should go to the Moon's mother, let her ask her son the Moon; at night he peeks with his moonlight into every hole and nook and cranny, through every groove and window. Perhaps he has seen such a bird somewhere."

gdjegod na svijetu u jednog kralja vrt, a u vrtu, visokim zidom ograđenu, u zlatnom kavezu pticu, koja nese zlatna jaja. Na vratima straže stražu dva lava, dva risa, dva mrka vuka, dva slona trbonoše. "Jesam," veli Sunce, "i to vidio sam u toga i toga kralja, u toj i toj zemlji." Kaže Sunce sve, što je i kako je.

Putnici nijesu mogli večerati sa Suncem, jer bi se spržili od teške žege, nego Sunčeva majka, zvijezda sunčanica, ispokoji goste i kaže im za kralja, u koga je ptica, što nese zlatna jaja. Sad junak momak ide sa svojom posestrimom u kraljevstvo onoga kralja. Kad dođu tamo, usiječe vila jedne noći u ponoći šibicu u šumi i dade je svom pobratimu, pak mu kaže: "Kad dođemo na vrata onoga vrta, gdje je ptica, biće ponoći; ja ću ti donijeti ključe od vrata, što ih svake noći sam kralj čuva pod svojim uzglavljem u svojoj postelji; ti ćes ovom šibicom šicnuti zvijeri, što stražu straže pred vratima, pak ćeš onda otključati vrata i ući u vrt." Tako i bude.

Vila ode oko ponoći u kraljeve dvore. Niko je ne vidi i ne čuje. Kralj spava. Vila se maši pod kraljevo uzglavlje i izvuče zlatan ključ od vrata, pa ga donese svome junaku. Kad pred vrata, slonovi budni, jedan s jedne drugi s druge strane, mašu njuškama i pušu kroz nozdrve. Junak momak prišunji se blizu, šicnu šibicom jednog i drugog slona. Obadva se okamene onaj čas, kad su podigli njuške, kako će junaka satrti. Poslije slonova stoje na straži mrki vuci, jedan s jedne a drugi s druge strane. Kad junak k njima, obadva iscere zube i poskoče k njemu. On brzo šicne šibicom jednoga i drugoga. Obadva se vuka okamene, kako su se već bili popeli na stražnje noge i od pedlja zinuli i zube iskesili.

Ide junak dalje. Eto ti dva ljuta risa, jedan s jedne a drugi s druge strane. Upravo u skoku na junaka kao mačka na miša. On ih brzo šicnu šibicom. Obadva se u skoku okamene. Upravo do vrata sjede dva lava, jedan s jedne a drugi s druge strane. Junak ne čeka da se lavovi podignu, nego pritrči, pak šicne šibicom i jednoga i drugoga. Obadva se lava okamene. Uzme junak zlatne ključe, otvori zlatnu bravu na vratima, uđe s posestrimom svojom u vrt, nađe u njem još i krilatu aždaju kod kaveza. I aždaju brzo šicnu šibicom, a ona se odmah okameni. Uzme kavez s pticom pod pazuho, a posestrima

The travelers stayed with the Wind's mother for the night, and the next day they went to seek the Moon's mother. When they arrived at her home, she kindly received them for the night. They had to wait a long time until the full Moon came home to its mother for supper. At supper the guests explained why they had come. The Moon thought and thought, and then said: "I have not seen such a bird anywhere; at least I don't remember. But you know what, go to the Sun's mother. Perhaps the Sun has seen such a bird somewhere."

The next day the hero and his fairy sister set out once again, this time in search of the Sun's mother. They arrived there at sunset. The Sun's mother received the guests for the night, but hid them in ice storage, so the Sun wouldn't fry and burn them. When the Sun came home to its mother for supper, the mother relayed the message of the guests, inquiring whether the Sun had seen anywhere in the world a king's garden surrounded by a high wall, and in the garden a golden cage with a bird that lays golden eggs. At the gate there would be two lions, two lynx, two unrelenting wolves, two huge elephants and two swift greyhounds standing guard. "Yes, I did see it," said the Sun, and he explained that he had seen it with such-and-such a king, in such-and-such a kingdom. The Sun described everything for them, just as it was.

The travelers could not dine with the Sun, because they would be burned from the heavy heat, but the Sun's mother, the Sun's star, informed the guests about the king who had such a bird which lays golden eggs. At once the young man, the hero, went with his fairy sister to the kingdom of that king. One night after they had arrived, the fairy sister lit a red-hot match in the forest and gave it to her brother, saying: "When I come to the door of that garden where the bird lives, it will be midnight, and I will bring the key which every night the king himself guards under the pillow on his bed. You will take the match, strike it on the beasts that stand guard in front of the door, and you will unlock the door and enter the garden." Thus it was.

About midnight the fairy sister went to the king's palace. No one saw her or heard her. The king was asleep. The fairy reached out under the king's

vila ogrne ga svojim maglenim plaštem. Kao da ga nosi vjetar, tako mu se učini.

Do zore stigne doma. Bijela vila obuče svoju gujsku košuljicu i ode pod postelju u ložnicu, a junak objesi zlatni kavez s pticom o klin i legne spavati. Kad jutrom probudi se i ustane, te gleda pticu u kavezu. Ptica snijela troje zlatnih jaja. Posestrima vila kaže junaku: "Nosi pticu kralju i prosi ga za kćer." Junak nosi pticu u zlatnom kavezu kralju. Kad kralj vidi pticu, što nese zlatna jaja, obraduje se, ali kad razumije, da momak prosi njegovu kćer za sebe, ne obraduje se, nego veli: "Ima još na svijetu jedan kralj, koji ima u svom vrtu krušku, na kojoj rode zlatne kruške. Ako želiš biti moj zet, a ti donesi onu krušku i presadi je u moj vrt."

Veseo otišao je junak u kraljev dvor, a tužan se povratio iz njega. Kaže sve, što je i kako je, svojoj posestrimi, a ona mu veli: "Nije kud, moramo opet ići propitati kod Vjetrove i kod Mjesečeve majke za kralja, u čijem vrtu raste kruška, na kojoj rode zlatne kruške."

Idu opet redom, kuda i prije. Ne mogu propitati ni u Vjetra, ni u Mjeseca, ni u Sunca. Čuju kod Sunčeve majke, kako bi dobro bilo, kad bi išli priupitati se kod Oblakove majke. I Oblak svuda prolazi i putuje po svijetu, možebit je on gdjegod vidio takvu krušku. Šta znadu drugo, nego put pod noge, pa hajde k Oblakovoj majci. Kad oni tamo, kaže im Oblak, da ne zna za takovu krušku. "Ali idite," veli, "k Vazduhovoj majci. Vazduh svuda putuje i ulazi po cijelom svijetu, možebit je on vidio takovu krušku."

Ide junak sa svojom posestrimom k Vazduhovoj majci. Vazduh im kaže za krušku, ali kad oni tamo, kruška pred kraljevim dvorom. Dvor je ograđen dvostrukim bedemom i trostrukim zidom. Na svakim vratima straže stražu zmajevi plameniti. Iz ralja im plamen liže. Štogod zadahnu, sve spale i otruju. U vrtu čuvaju zmije drvolazi krušku. Po zidu okolo vrta sjede orlušine i kanjuzi, sve veći od većega i grđi od grđega, i jato kobaca i piuljača, kokošara i golubara.

Posestrima vila ode u planinu i pozove u pomoć vile rojenice i vjetrenice, poledice i vilovnjake. Vile vjetrenice podignu vjetrinu i oluju, poledice

pillow, pulled out the golden key to the door and took it to her hero. But, in front of the door, the huge elephants were awake, one on one side, the other on the other side; they swung their trunks and expelled air through their nostrils. The young hero approached closer, struck one elephant, and then the other, with the match. Both of them turned to stone at the very moment that they were going to crush the hero. Next to the elephants, stern wolves stood guard, one on one side, the other on the other side. When the hero came closer, both of them bared their teeth and leapt towards him. He quickly frightened away one and then the other with the match. Both wolves turned to stone just as they were, up on their hind legs with open jaws and bared teeth. The hero went further. There were two angry lynx, one on one side, the other on the other side. They jumped onto the hero just as a cat would pounce on a mouse. He quickly struck each one with the match. Both of them turned to stone in flight. Just by the door sat two lions, one on one side, the other on the other side. The hero did not wait for the lions to rise, but ran toward them and struck one and the other with the match. Both lions turned to stone. The hero took the golden keys, unlocked the door with the golden keyhole, entered the garden with his fairy sister and, once inside, found a winged dragon near the cage. Quickly he struck the dragon with the match, and it immediately turned to stone. The hero took the bird in its cage under his arm, and the fairy sister covered him with her thick cape. He felt as if the wind were carrying him.

By dawn he arrived home. The white fairy put on her viper skin and went under the bed in the bedroom, while the hero hung the golden cage with the bird on a peg and went to sleep. In the morning he awoke, got up and saw the bird in the cage. The bird had laid three golden eggs. The fairy sister said to the hero: "Take the bird to the king and ask for his daughter's hand." The hero took the bird in the golden cage to the king. When the king saw the bird that lays golden eggs, he was glad, but when he remembered that the young man sought his daughter for himself, he was not happy at all and said: "There is a king in the world somewhere who has in his garden a pear tree on which

zamijese led. Digne se strašna olujina, led sune iz oblaka, pobjegnu orlušine i kanjuzi i sve ptice grabilice, zmaj se zavuče pod svoju škulju pod bedemom. Zmije drvolazi uvuku se u svoje jame. Vilovnjaci upregnu se za olujinu, pak late stablo kruškovo, iščupaju s korijenjem iz zemlje i prenesu za živi čas oko ponoći iz jedne zemlje u drugu, iz jednog kraljevstva u drugo. Brzo iskopaju jamu u vrtu i presade krušku.

Sjutradan ode juank momak do kralja, pa ga vodi u vrt, da mu pokaže krušku, na kojoj rode zlatne kruške. Kralj se obraduje, ali odmah reče junaku: "Ima još na svijetu jedan kralj, koji čuva u srebrnoj staji ovna vitoroga, na kome raste zlatna vuna, iz koje se prede i tka zlatno tkanje. Dok mi ne dobaviš onoga ovna, nećeš biti moj zet." Junak se tužan povrati od kralja i kaže svojoj posestrimi, što kralj sada opete zanovijeta.

Posestrima vila vodi opet junaka svoga pobratima k Vjetrovoj majci. Ništa ne zna Vjetar za ovna. Vodi ga k Mjesečevoj majci. Ni Mjesec ne zna za ovna, na kome raste zlatna vuna. Idu Vazduhovoj majci. Vazduh im kaže, neka idu k Moru i pitaju More za ovna. Vazduhu se čini, da je vidio ovna na jednom otoku u Moru, ali pravo ne zna gdje. Ide junak sa svojom posestrimom k Moru. More kaže: "Hajdete sa mnom, dovešću vas k onom otoku, gdje ima kralj u srebrnoj staji ovna, na kome raste zlatna vuna. Daleko je to."

Junak ide sa svojom posestrimom. More ih vodi. Dugo putuju. Kad dođu do onoga otoka, obala je strma oko cijelog otoka; ne može je ptica preletjeti. Bijela vila uze svoga pobratima za ruku i uzleti na obalu. Kad oni na otok do kraljeva dvora, ali oko srebrne staje jezero, na njem samo jedan čamac kraljev. Čamac je privezan uz srebrn stupac na obali, srebrnim lancem i zlatnim lokotom zaključan. Čuvaju ga tri kraljeve sluge s golim sabljama.

Posestrima vila kaže junaku: "Hajdemo s druge strane." Uzme vila orahovu ljupinu i iz nje postane čamac. Vila rastre svoj plašt i postane jedro. Uzme iglu ispod svoga grla, kojom je skopčala svoj bijeli ogrtač, a iz igle postane veslo. Sjednu pobratim i posestrima u čamac, prevezu se preko jezera do srebrne staje. Uzmu ovna, svežu ga za rogove junačkim pojasom i vode ga do Mora. More prebaci putnike na drugu obalu. Junak momak dovede sjutra

golden pears grow. If you want to be my son-in-law, bring me that pear tree and plant it in my garden."

The hero had gone to the king's palace joyful, but he returned saddened. He told everything to his fairy sister, and she said: "There is no way out, we must go again and ask the Wind's and the Moon's mother where to find the king who has a pear tree with golden pears on it."

They went exactly the same way as before. They did not find an answer from the Wind, nor from the Moon, nor from the Sun. The Sun's mother said that it would be good to ask the Cloud's mother. The Cloud had been everywhere and had traveled the world; perhaps it had seen such a pear tree somewhere. What could they do but go and seek the Cloud's mother? When they arrived, the Cloud said it knew nothing of such a pear tree, but he suggested: "Do go to the Air's mother. The Air travels everywhere and goes into every part of the world; perhaps it has seen such a pear tree."

And so the hero and his fairy sister went to the Air's mother. The Air told them about the pear tree, and when they arrived at the king's palace, there was a pear tree in front of the palace. The palace was surrounded by a double fortress and a triple wall. At all the doors fiery dragons were on guard. Flames shot out from their jaws, and their breath burned and poisoned everything nearby. In the garden, tree creeper snakes enveloped the pear tree. On the wall surrounding the garden, eagles and other birds of prey sat, one bigger than the other and one uglier than the other, and flocks of sparrow hawks, hen harriers and pigeon hawks.

The fairy sister went into the mountains and called to other fairies to help her: a swarm of water and wind fairies, bitter frost fairies, and sorcerer fairies. Wind fairies raised the wind and storms. Black frost furrowed its brow and a terrible storm began: ice balls fell from the clouds; the eagles and all birds of prey flew away; the dragon hid in his hole under the bulwark; tree snakes, too, slithered into their holes. The sorcerers harnessed the storm and enveloped the pear tree, pulled it out of the earth with its roots and

kralju, ocu ljepote djevojke, ovna, na kome raste zlatna vuna, iz koje se prede i tka zlatno tkanje.

Kralj se obraduje, ali mu još nije dosta, nego veli junaku: "Ako želiš biti moj zet, a ti vidiš eno onaj kameniti brijeg i onaj do ispod njega. Ako mi ovaj brijeg do sutra ne izravnaš s dolom, i ako po ravnici ne postane ledina, dok ja sjutra iz postelje ustanem, nećeš mi biti zet."

Junak se tuži svojoj posestrimi, a ona ga tješi, i odmah ode u planinu, te zove vile, svoje druge, na mobu. Dođe moba i raskopa do zore cijeli onaj brijeg i izravna ga s dolinom i zasadi ledinom.

Kad sjutra ustane kralj, ne ima brijega, sva je ravnica obrasla ledinom. Kralj kaže: "I to je lijepo, ali ako do sjutra ne sagradiš na onoj ravnici usred sredine bijele dvore kraljevske, a u njima toliko soba koliko je dana u godini, i sve sobe lijepo namještene po gospodski, nećeš biti moj zet." Junak kaže posestrimi što kralj zanovijeta. Opet zove vila sve svoje druge na mobu. Do zore saziću bijele dvore od sivca kamena, i sve namjeste gospodski. Takve dvore ne ima nijedan kralj na svijetu, kakve su za noć sazidale vile.

Kad sjutradan šeće se kralj s junakom po bijelim dvorovima. Još kralju nešto nedostaje; otvara prozore i gleda po polju, pak veli junaku: "Vidi, ono pusto polje na ravnici. Ako do sjutra ono polje, koliko je dugo i široko, ne iskrčiš, ne uzoreš, ne posiješ bjelicom pšenicom, pak tu pšenicu sjutra ne požanješ, ne ovršiš, ne oviješ, ne samelješ i pogaču od nje za ručak ne umijesiš i ispečeš, nećeš biti moj zet."

Kad to čuje junak momak, rastuži se i ražali se više no ikad. To barem svako zna, da nije moguće uraditi. Tuži se junak svojoj posestrimi. Ona mu veli: "Pobratime, i u to ćemo zadrijeti, te sreću pokušati mobom. Ako svi pozvanici dođu, može nešto biti. Ako ne dođu, silom ništa."

Ide vila posestrima brže od vjetra po planinama i ravnicama i zove na mobu sve vile i vilovnjake: rojenice, poledice, vjetrenice i ljutice. U prvi mrak već vrve po poljani poslenici kao mravi. Polje za čas iskrčeno, za čas uzorano, posijano i do dana sve gotovo. Na polju talaskaju se slogovi zrele pšenice, ljepota je gledati. Kralj došao u polje da vidi neviđeno. Do podne žito požnjeto,

transferred it before midnight from one soil to the other, from one kingdom to the other. Quickly they dug a hole in the garden and replanted the pear tree.

The next day the young hero went again to the king and took him to the garden to show him the pear tree on which were golden pears. The king was pleased, but immediately told the hero: "There is a king in the world somewhere who keeps in his stable a ram with twisted antlers, on which golden wool grows, and from which a golden weave is spun. Unless you bring me that ram, you will not be my son-in-law." The hero returned from the king sad and told his fairy sister that the king was still unsatisfied.

Fairy sister again took her hero brother to the Wind's mother. The Wind knew nothing about the ram. He took them to the Moon's mother. Neither did the Moon know anything about the ram on whose antlers golden wool grows, and said: "Go to the Air's mother." The Air told them to go to the Sea and ask the Sea about the ram. The Air thought it had seen a ram on one of the islands in the Sea, but did not know where. And so the hero and his fairy sister went to the Sea. The Sea said: "Come with me, and I will take you to an island where a king has a silver stable with a ram that grows golden wool. The place is far from here."

The hero went with his fairy sister, and the Sea showed them the way. They traveled for a long time. When they arrived at the island, the entire perimeter was steep and rugged. Not even a bird could fly over it. The white fairy took her brother by the hand and flew upward onto the seashore. Once on the island, they went to the king's palace, but around the golden stable was a lake, and on it only one boat, the king's. The boat was chained to a silver post with a silver chain and secured by a golden lock. It was guarded by three of the king's guards, each with a drawn saber.

The fairy sister told the hero: "Let's go from the other side." The fairy took a walnut shell and it turned into a boat. The fairy spread her cape and it turned into a sail. She took a pin from under her throat with which she hooked her white cape, and it turned into an oar. They climbed into the boat and went

ovršeno, ovijeno, brašno samljeveno, pogača umiješena i za ručak ispečena. No vile ljutice umiješale među pšenicu ljulja. Vila posestrima od silnoga posla nije baš mogla dospjeti svuda, te pripaziti na sve, ali opomene junaka pobratima, da ne jede odmah od pečene pogače.

Kralj pozove junaka na ručak. Oni sjednu za sto. Kralj razlomi pogaču, a ona se dimi od vrelosti. Jede kralj u slast pogaču i najede se. Glava ga zaboli, muka ga uhvati, zlo mu je, pa zlo još i gore. Otrovao se vrućom pogačom, pa umro. Junak se oženi ljepotom djevojkom, kraljevom kćerkom, i postane kralj. Sad je lijepo živio. Imao je ljepotu kraljicu; imao pticu u zlatnom kavezu što nese zlatna jaja; imao je nadalje u svom vrtu krušku, na kojoj rode zlatne kruške; imao je napokon ovna vitoroga, na kom raste vuna zlatna, iz koje se prede i tka zlatno tkanje. Samo jedno zlo je imao, u žitu mu rodio kukolj.

by water to the silver stable. They took the ram and tied his antlers with the hero's belt and took him to the Sea. The Sea took them to the other side. The next morning the young hero took the ram, on which golden wool grows and from which is spun and woven a golden fabric, to the king, father of the beautiful maiden.

The king was happy, but he still wanted more and said to the hero: "If you wish to be my son-in-law, look at that stone hill over there and what is below it. If you don't level the hill with the valley below by tomorrow, and if in the morning the valley is not grass turf when I get up, you will not be my son-in-law." The hero complained to his fairy sister, and she consoled him and immediately went to the hills to call her fairy companions to help with the work. The fairy helpers came and by dawn dug up the whole hill and evened it out with the valley and planted grass.

By the time the king was up in the morning, there was no hill and in its place was a plain covered with grass turf. The king said: "And this is beautiful, but if by next morning you do not build in the middle of this plain white royal palaces, in which there are as many rooms as there are days in a year, and all the rooms furnished royally, you will not be my son-in-law." The hero told his fairy sister that the king still grumbles. The fairy again called on her other companions to help build. Until dawn they built white castles from grey stone, and everything was furnished royally. Not one king in the world had such palaces as the fairies built overnight.

The next morning the king went with the hero into the white castles. Something was still lacking for the king. He opened the windows and looked at the fields and said to the hero: "Look at that empty field in the valley – if by morning you don't clear that field as it is long and wide, plough it and sow white wheat, what you reap you thresh and twist, and from it make and bake flat bread, you will not be my son-in-law."

When the young hero heard this, he became sad, sadder than ever. This, everyone knows, is impossible to do. He complained to his fairy sister. She tells him: "Blood brother, we'll get into this too, and seek happiness with fairy

helpers. If all called come, there will be something. If they don't, there'll be nothing by force."

Faster than the wind went the fairy sister to the hills and the valleys and called all fairies and sorcerers for help: water, wind, and field fairies, and vipers. By dusk the workers swarmed like ants in the field. In an hour the field was cleared, plowed, sowed, and by daylight all was done. The field had filled plentifully with ripe wheat. It was a beauty to see, a wonder. The king came to the field to see what had never been seen before. By noon the grain was reaped, threshed, twisted, ground into flour, made into flat bread and baked in time for lunch. But the angry fairies had mixed into the wheat some cockle-weed. Fairy sister wasn't able to be everywhere and watch over everything, but she warned her hero brother not to immediately eat the baked flat bread.

The king called the hero to lunch. They sat at the table. The king broke the bread and it steamed from heat. The king ate the flat bread with gusto and had his fill. His head began to hurt, and he began to feel sick, nauseated, and worse. He was poisoned by the steaming hot flat bread and died. The hero married the beautiful maiden, the king's daughter, and became king. He lived well. He had a beautiful queen. He had a bird in a golden cage that laid golden eggs, he had a pear tree which bore golden pears in his garden, and, finally, he had a ram with twisted antlers on which golden wool grew, which could be spun and woven into golden fabric. In the end he had only one misfortune: in his wheat field grew corn cockle.

How The Hedgehog Married

Kako Se Je Jež Oženio

KAKO SE JE JEŽ OŽENIO

Jednom su bili jedan muž i žena, bili su vrlo siromašni, ništa nisu imali kod kuće osim jednoga prasca i jednu prasicu. Oni nisu imali nikakva djeteta, pa su uvijek dragoga Boga molili da bi im dao dijete, pa bilo ono kao jež. Ona je doista zanijela, za devet mjeseci rodila i rodila je ježa. Taj jež nije govorio ništa, tek kad mu je bilo sedam godina stade govoriti. Otac je jednom jadikovao da mu nema tko prasce pasti. To čuo taj sin jež, pa je ocu rekao da ide on na pašu sa prascima.

Otac i majka podigli su prema nebu ruke i zahvalili se Bogu: "Hvala Bogu, koji je dao da nam je sin stao govoriti!" Otac ga je poslao sa prascima odmah u šumu. U šumi je bio šesnaest godina i nitko nije znao gdje je. Otac i majka su uvijek njega tražili i plakali za njim.

U šesnaestoj godini išla su jednom dva grofa u lov, pa su zalutali u toj šumi. Nikako nisu mogli naći puta. Najednom su čuli gdje cvile prasci i oni pošli prema onom kraju odakle je bilo čuti prasce. Tamo nije bilo čovjeka, već sami prasci. Stali su oni dozivati pastira i došao je pred njih jež. On ih je upitao što ovdje traže i što bi rado. Oni su mu odgovorili, da su u šumi zalutali i da ne znaju sada iz nje izaći. Jež je jednome od njih rekao: "Gospodine, vi imate tri kćeri, pa ako mi date jednu od njih za ženu, ja ću vas odvesti na pravi put!" Taj je grof stao razmišljati i napokon zaključio da je bolje da mu obeća jednu kćer za ženu, nego da pogine u šumi, pa mu je rekao: "Koju god ćeš odabrati, dat ću ti je!" I tako je jež izveo ova dva grofa iz šume.

Kad su grofovi otiši, spremi se on sa svojim prascima na sajam, samo

HOW THE HEDGEHOG MARRIED

*O*nce there lived a husband and wife who were very poor. They had nothing at home except for a hog and a sow. They didn't have any children, so they prayed all the time that God would give them a child, even if it were a hedgehog. The wife indeed conceived and after nine months gave birth – to a hedgehog. The hedgehog did not speak at all until it was seven years old. One day the father was complaining that he had no one who could tend the hogs. The hedgehog heard this and said he would go to pasture with the hogs.

The father and mother lifted their arms toward the sky and thanked God: "Thank you, Lord, that our son speaks." The father immediately sent him off to the forest with the hogs. For sixteen years the hedgehog was in the forest and no one knew where he was. The father and mother endlessly looked for and cried for him.

One day in that sixteenth year, two young counts went hunting in the forest and got lost. No matter how hard they searched, they could not find their path. Suddenly they heard hogs whining. They followed the sound and found no human there, only hogs. They began to call out for the herdsman, and the hedgehog came to them. He asked them what they were doing and what they wanted. The counts told the hedgehog they were lost in the forest and that they didn't know how to get out of it. The hedgehog said to one of them: "Good sir, I have heard that you have three daughters, and if you give me one as a wife, I will take you to the right path." The count thought for a while and finally decided that it is better to promise one daughter as a wife

dva je ostavio u šumi. Na sajmu je dobro svoje prasce prodao i kupio konje i kočiju i zapovjedio kočijašu da ga ima odvesti u grad, gdje su bila ona dva grofa. On se je onamo dovezao, a kad je grofov sluga opazio da je kočija stala pred grofovskim dvorom priskočio je brzo do kočije, da će gospodi pomoći sići. Ali kada je sluga kočiju otvorio, skočio je iz kočije jež i odmah ušao u dvor i po stubama u gornji kat. Došao je pred onoga grofa i upitao ga da li će mu sada dati ono što mu je obećao. Grof mu je odgovorio: "Idi i upitaj ih, da li te hoće koja!"

On je upitao najprije najstariju, a ona mu se samo jako narugala. Upitao je i drugu, srednju, ali i ta ga je otpravila kao i ona najstarija. Konačno je upitao i onu najmlađu. Ona nije htjela ništa reći, nego se je samo smijala. U večer su svi večerali i jež s njima. Poslije večere su išle te gospodične spavati, a jež se zavukao toj najmlađoj pod krevet. Kad je ona zaspala, svukao je on svoju kožu, pa je postao prelijepi mladić u zlatnoj opravi. U jutro, kad se ona probudila, opipa oko sebe i opazi kraj sebe prelijepa mladića u zlatnoj opravi, od koje je cijela soba sjala.

Drugi dan, kad se je taj mladić ustao, obukao je opet svoju kožu, pa je bio jež. Ona ga je cio dan u rukama nosila i u gubicu ljubila. Još istoga dana su išli župniku i ondje najavili svoje vjenčanje. Sestre su je jako psovale jer im veliku sramotu radi.

Za nekoliko dana došao je jež k svojoj zaručnici i otišli su u crkvu da ih župnik vjenča. Sada su je opet sestre jako psovale, čak su je i tukle, jedva je utekla da je nisu ubile. Kad su došli pred žrtvenik, rekao je on njoj da kad će im župnik ruke vezati, neka ona onom drugom rukom isčupa jednu bodlju iz njegova hrpta, pa da će postati mladić. Ona je tako učinila. Kad je ona isčupala bodlju, jež je odmah postao prelijepi mladić u zlatnoj opravi i cijela je crkva od njegova odijela zasjala.

Kad su se vraćali kući iz crkve gledale su sestre njezine, ali nisu vidjele sada ježa, već prelijepa mladića u zlatnoj opravi. Tako su došli oni kući, a one dvije sestre su sada jako žalile i plakale što ga nisu uzele za muža jedna ili druga, tim više što su vidjele da ima i mnogo novaca.

than to die in the forest, so he said: "Whichever you choose, I will give her to you!" And so the hedgehog led the two counts out of the forest.

When the counts left, the hedgehog prepared his hogs to go to market, leaving only two in the forest. At the market he sold the hogs for a good price and bought horses and a carriage. He told the carriage driver to take him to the city where the two counts lived. When the carriage arrived, the count's servant noticed it and ran up to help the guests descend. But as the servant opened the door of the carriage, the hedgehog jumped out, and immediately went into the court and up the staircase to the second floor. He came before the count who had promised him his daughter and asked him if he was going to keep his word. The count answered: "Go to them and see if one of them wants you."

The hedgehog first asked the eldest daughter, and she ridiculed him. Next, he asked the middle daughter, and this one sent him off as well. He finally asked the youngest daughter. She did not want to say anything at all and only smiled. In the evening everyone dined together with the hedgehog. After dinner the maidens went to sleep, and the hedgehog hid under the bed of the youngest one. When she fell asleep, he took off his skin and turned into a beautiful young man in golden attire. In the morning when she woke up, she discovered that a handsome young man in golden attire that lit up the whole room was next to her.

The next day, when the youth got up, he again put on his skin and turned into a hedgehog. She carried him all day in her arms and kissed his snout. The very same day they went to the parish and arranged to be married. The sisters scolded her because she was disgracing them all.

Within several days' time the hedgehog came for his fiancée, but the sisters again scolded her; they even beat her so badly that she barely escaped with her life. Then the hedgehog and the maiden went to the church to be married.

As the couple came before the altar, the hedgehog told her that once the priest binds their hands together, she should pull one quill from his back with

Na piru je bilo sve veselo, osobito mladenci, i ja sam bio tamo, a jer nisam bio pozvan otjerali su me u kuhinju, gdje je kuharica uzela lopatu i njom me otraga gurnula, da sam odmah odletio u Ravnu goru.

the other arm, and he would turn into a young man. She did just that. When she pulled the quill, the hedgehog immediately became a most handsome young man in golden attire, and the whole church glistened from the radiance of his clothes.

While the newly married couple was returning home from the church, the two older sisters were expecting to see the hedgehog. Instead, a wonderful young man in golden attire arrived home with their sister. Upon seeing the couple, the two sisters became very sad. They cried since both of them had rejected him, especially now that they knew he was as wealthy as he was handsome.

At the wedding feast everybody made merry, especially the young couple, and I was there. But, because I was not invited, I was pushed into the kitchen where the cook took a spade and hit me with it from behind so hard that I immediately flew to Flat Hill.

How Witches Married
A Lazy Maiden To A Count

Kako Su Vještice
Udale Lijenu Djevojku Za Grofa

KAKO SU VJEŠTICE UDALE LIJENU DJEVOJKU ZA GROFA

Tako je bila jedna mati i imala je jednu kćer, koja nije htjela nikada ništa presti ni raditi, i zato se nije mogla nikako udati. Ta je mati imala mnogo, mnogo prediva i sve je ležalo i kvarilo se, jer ga nije imao tko urediti. Ta je cura imala tri tete vještice i žao im je bilo prediva, pa su rekle materi te djevojke, svojoj sestri: "Muči, muči, sestro, mi ćemo noćas dovesti naše družice, pa ćemo sve predivo tvoje ispresti!"

Te su njezine sestre bile prave pravcate vještice i one su prijeko noći sabrale svoje družice i došle su k svojoj sestri i, što je bilo u večer predivo, to je ujutro bila preda.

Nedaleko te matere bio je grofovski dvor i u njemu mladi grof. Mati se je svuda hvalila sa svojom kćeri i pred tim se mladim grofom hvalila, da koliko je njezina kći u jednu noć isprela. Na to poče razmišljati mladi grof: "Kad ona tako rado prede, isprest će i moje. I ja imam mnogo prediva!" I na to ju je on uzeo k sebi i vjenčao se s njome. Ali kad tamo, kad se ona vjenčala, nije htjela ništa presti. Nagovori je mati da pozove k sebi svoje tete pa da će joj one već pomoći i da je ne će više muž tjerati da prede.

Sabere ona doista te svoje tete u goste i tomu se mladomu grofu nisu one ništa sviđale. Jedna je teta imala jako dugačak nos, druga je teta imala jako velike zube, a treća je teta imala jako široku stražnjicu. I upita ih taj mladi grof: "Što je vama, tete moje, da ste tako ružne?" Na to mu odgovori ona koja je imala jako dugačak nos: "Joj, sinko moj, mi po cijele noći predemo, mi

HOW WITCHES MARRIED A LAZY MAIDEN TO A COUNT

*T*here once lived a mother who had a daughter who never wanted to spin or do anything, and that is why she could never get married. That mother had a lot of wool but everything just lay there and was spoiling, because there was no one to put it in order. The daughter had three aunts, the witches, and they felt sorry for the rotting fiber, so they said to the mother of this girl, their sister: "Do not worry, sister, we will bring our friends tonight, and we will spin all of your fiber."

Those sisters were real witches and during the night they rounded up their friends and came to their sister and, what was at night fiber, by morning became yarn.

Not far from this mother's home was a count's castle, and in it lived a young count. The mother boasted everywhere about her daughter and in front of that young count praised her, as to how much her daughter spun in one night. Then the young count began to think: "When she so willingly spins, she could spin mine too, and I have a lot of fiber!" And so he took the girl and married her. But then, when she was married, she did not want to spin. Her mother convinced her to call her aunts for help so the husband would no longer pressure her to spin.

Indeed, the bride brought her aunts for a visit, but the young count did not find them pleasing. One aunt had a terribly long nose, the second one had terribly large teeth, and the third aunt had a terribly large behind. And the

moramo biti ružne. Ja moram imati dug nos, sad ga s jednom rukom nategnem, sada s drugom, dok predem, i tako mi je postao dugačak nos!" Zatim mu je rekla ona koja je imala velike zube: "Joj, sinko moj, mi po cijele noći predemo, mi moramo biti ružne. Ja moram imati velike zube, kad vučem zubima cijele noći kudelju nategnem si zube!" Posljednja mu je rekla ona koja je imala jako široku stražnjicu: "Joj, sinko moj, mi po cijele noći predemo, mi moramo biti ružne. Ja moram imati jako široku stražnjicu, kad dugo predem i pomičem se amo-tamo po krevetu, pa si raširim stražnjicu!"

Uplašio se taj grofovski sin da će i njegova žena postati tako ružnom ako prede i nije je htio više nikada tjerati da prede.

Tako su ove tri tete vještice udale lijenu djevojku za grofa i još joj pomogle da nije trebala presti.

young count asked them: "What is the matter with you, my aunts, that you are so ugly?" Then the one with the long nose answered him: "Oh, my son, we spin the whole night, we must be ugly. I have to have a long nose, for now with one hand I stretch it, now with the other, while I spin. And that's how my nose became so long." Then the aunt with big teeth said: "Oh, my son, we spin all night long, we have to be ugly. I have to have big teeth, for when I pull fiber with my teeth all night, I stretch my teeth!" And the last aunt with the large behind said: "Oh, my son, we spin the whole night, we have to be ugly. I have to have a very large behind, for when I spin for a long time and move here-and-there over the bed, I stretch my behind!"

The count got frightened that his wife would also become ugly if she were to spin, and so he no longer forced his wife to spin.

And thus these three aunts, the witches, married a lazy maiden to a count and even helped her so that she would not have to spin.

How A Young Man Married A Snake

Kako Je Jedan Mladić Oženio Zmiju

KAKO JE JEDAN
MLADIĆ OŽENIO ZMIJU

Neka je majka imala devet sinova, a među njima jednoga bedastoga, ili boje, ljudi su ga držali bedastim. Taj bedasti sin slao svoju majku da ide prositi za njega grofovu kćer. Njegova se majka isprva skanjivala, ali je ipak pošla i došla k grofu. Kad ju je grof opazio, rekao je kuharici: "Daj ovoj nesreći nešto pojesti, i gledaj da ovu prosjakinju što prije iz kuće spraviš!" Kuharica joj je dala, a kad je starica pojela otišla je vrlo žalosna, a da nije grofu ni spomenula po što je došla.

Dođe ona kući i reče sinu: "Ajde, ti moj sinko s Bogom, ti si velik bedak, kako bih ja za tebe prosila grofovu kćer, kad su mi ondje rekli, da sam prosjakinja!" Ali sin joj nije htio vjerovati, nego joj je rekao: "Ajte vi majko, samo još jednom, vi niste prvi put dobro prosili!"

I tako je ona opet pošla k grofu. Grof ju je baš opazio kroz prozor kad je dolazila k njemu, pa je stao odmah vikati nad njom: "Evo, opet dolazi ona prosjakinja!" Dođe u kuhinju kad je ona onamo došla pa se izdere nad kuharicom i reče: "Daj joj štogod, samo da što prije otiđe!" – Ali ona nije htjela otići nego je rekla grofu: " Ja bih rada, gospodine grofe, s vama nešto razgovarati pa se pravo ne usuđujem!" Reče joj on: "A što bi ti rado razgovarala?"

Ona mu na to odgovori: "Moj me sin napastuje da bih vas prosila da bi vi obećali svoju kćer njemu za ženu!"

Reče joj on: "Ajde, ti ludo, kako možeš samo misliti da bih obećao i dao svoju kćer za tvoga sina!" Dali su joj ondje nešto jesti i piti pa je opet otišla kući.

HOW A YOUNG MAN
MARRIED A SNAKE

A mother had nine sons, and among them a blockhead, or rather, people took him for a fool. This foolish son sent his mother to ask for him the hand of a count's daughter. When the count saw her, he said to the cook: "Give this poor woman something to eat, and see to it you send this beggar off as soon as possible." The cook fed her and, when she had eaten, she left very sad that she did not mention anything to the count.

She got home and said to her son: "Be with God, my son, you are a big fool; how could I ask for the count's daughter, when they told me there that I was a beggar!" But the son did not want to believe her, and said to her: "Go, my mother, only once more. You did not ask correctly the first time."

And so she went again to see the count. The count saw her through the window when she was approaching, and immediately began to shout at her: "Here comes that beggar again!" He goes to the kitchen when she got there and shouted to the cook: "Give her something, so she will leave sooner!" But she did not want to leave and said to the count: "I would like, Mr. Count, to talk with you about something, but I dare not!" He says to her: "And what would you like to talk to me about?"

To that she replied: "My son insists I ask you to promise your daughter to be his wife!"

He replies: "You fool, how could you even think that I would promise my daughter to your son?" They gave her something to eat and drink and again she went home.

Dođe ona kući i reče sinu sve kako joj je grof rekao. Na to se je sin jako razljutio i rekao majci: "Specite vi meni majko kruh, pa si idem sada sam tražiti ženu, ja si je negdje moram naći, makar da isprosim sebi za ženu i ljutu zmiju!"

Spekla mu mati kruha i on je otišao tražiti po svijetu ženu. Išao je nekakvim grmljem i u tomu je grmlju bila ljuta zmija. Izašla je ona pred njega i javila se njemu. On se je ljuto nad njom izderao: "Miči mi se s puta, ljuta zmijo!" Ona mu je na to odgovorila: "Ne ću ti se micati! Ti si rekao, da ćeš uzeti za ženu ljutu zmiju. Ja sam evo došla, ti sada mene moraš uzeti za ženu!" On se jako uplašio pa ju je uzeo sve od straha za ženu. Kad je to ona opazila, reče mu: "Ajde, ludo, što se ti mene bojiš! Ti ćeš po meni postati sretan!"

On je ženu doveo kući. Kad su se u kući smjestili, reče mu ona: "Sada uzmi konje i kola, pa hajdemo zajedno do moga doma!" Upregao je on konje u velika kola i odvezli su se k njezinu domu. Vozili su se daleko po svakojakim putovima dok su prispjeli do njezina doma. Ovdje su nametali puna kola i srebra i zlata i odveli sve to k njegovu domu.

Sada su istom priredili kod njega pir. Za stolom su sjedili gosti, a među njima on, momak i ona, ljuta zmija. Žene su među sobom govorile: " Bože moj, Bože moj, kako će on spavati sa zmijom!" Kada su išli njih dvoje u sobu spavati, išle su žene na otvor ključanice gledati kako će on sa zmijom spavati. Na svoje su najveće čudo opazile da je zmija skinula svoju zmijsku kožu i postala prelijepa djevojka, kakve nema pod suncem Božjim. Tu je kožu spremila pod prag i legla je onako prelijepa k njemu u krevet. Te su joj babe, kad su oni zaspali, ukrale zmijsku kožu i bacile u peć.

Kad se je sutradan u jutro ta prelijepa žena ustala i htjela se u svoju kožu obući i kad je nije mogla nigdje naći, počela je plakati i bila je žalosna cio dan. Proklinjala je babe: "Aj, vi vražje babe, što ste vi meni učinile! Meni će danas moje drugarice silan dar donijeti, a ja ga ne ću bez zmijske kože moći od njih primiti!" Uvečer su doista došle silne zmije i donijele njoj mnogo zlata i srebra. Dugo su cvilile i plakale da gdje je njihova družica. Ona je sve to čula, ali nije si mogla pomoći, jer nije imala u čemu među njih doći. Dugo su

She came home and told her son everything that the count told her. At that, the son got very angry and told his mother: "Bake me some bread, mother, and I will go alone to find myself a wife. I need to find a wife somewhere, even if it be an angry snake as a wife.

His mother baked him some bread and he left to find in this world a wife. He passed by some bushes and in a bush was an angry snake. She came out and appeared before him. He became angry at it and shouted: "Move out of the way, you angry snake!" She replied to him: "I will not move! You said you would take an angry snake as a wife. So here I am and you must take me for a wife!" He got frightened and out of fear took her as his wife. When she noticed that, she said: "You, fool, why do you fear me? You will be happy with me!"

He brought his wife home. When they settled in, she says to him: "Now take the horses and a cart, and let us go together to my home!" He harnessed horses to a big cart and they went to her home. They drove on all kinds of roads until they reached her home. There they filled the cart with silver and gold and drove everything to his home.

Once there, they prepared a celebration for them. At the table sat guests, and among them he, the young man, and she, the angry snake. The women talked among themselves: "My God, my God, how will he sleep with a snake!" When the two of them went to a room to sleep, the women flocked at the door to peek through the keyhole to see how will he sleep with a snake. At their biggest suprise they noticed that the snake took off its snake skin and became the most beautiful maiden, such that had not been seen under the holy Sun. She placed the skin at the threshold and, so beautifully, she lay down next to him in bed. When they fell asleep, those women stole the snake skin and threw it into the fire.

When the next day this most beautiful woman got up and wanted to put on her skin, and when she could not find it anywhere, she began to weep and was sad all day. She cursed the old women: "Oh, you devil's women, what did you do to me! Today my friends will bring me wonderful gifts, and I will

je čekale, konačno su odnijele natrag sve zlato i srebro, jer je nisu prepoznale.

Tako su je te babe doista prikratile za bogati dar, ali ona je ostala zato zauvijek lijepa i živjela je sretno, dobro i veselo s tim bedastim sinom do svoje smrti.

not be able to receive anything from them without my skin." In the evening mighty snakes really came and brought her a lot of gold and silver. For a long time they squealed and cried out, where could their friend be? She heard all this, but could not help herself because she did not have anything to put on and appear before them. They waited for a long time, and finally took back all the silver and gold, because they did not recognize her.

And so the women really denied her rich gifts, but instead, she remained beautiful forever and lived well happily and joyfully with that fool of a son until her death.

King's Daughter

Kraljeva Kći

KRALJEVA KĆI

Živio jednom jedan kralj koji je imao jako lijepu kćer. K njoj su dolazili prosci – mladi kraljevići – ali ih je ona sve odbijala, jer se zagledala u nekog lijepog pastira koji je lijepo pjevao i svirao. Kraljeva je kći svaki dan išla u šumu vidjeti pastira.

Jednoga dana čak dođe pastiru i reče mu: "Ja sam kraljeva kći. Moj bi otac htio da se vjenčam s kraljevićem, ali ja to neću, jer sam se u tebe zaljubila i s tobom bih se htjela vjenčati. Radi toga sam došla danas k tebi, da ti to kažem i da te pitam pristaješ li na to?" – Čuvši to, pastir se prestraši, skupi ovce i pobjegne kući.

Uskoro preko kraljevstva priđe silna vojska. Kralja i njegovu obitelj tuđa vojska zarobi, a mladu kraljevnu zatvore u visoku tvrđavu. Neprijatelj reče da će se s kraljevnom vjenčati samo onaj koji bude toliko hrabar i pametan da je izbavi iz tvrđave, te da će on naslijediti i njezino kraljevstvo. Mnogi su kraljevići pokušavali spasiti kraljevu kćer, ali ni jedan nije uspio. Kraljevnu je čuvao zmaj sa sedam glava koji je zaklao svakoga tko ju je pokušao spasiti.

Pastir dozna što se dogodilo s kraljevom kćeri i sjeti se kako mu je jednom rekla da bi se s njim vjenčala. Odluči ju spasiti. No prije nego je pošao, načini lijepu sviralu od ljeskove jednogodišnje mladice. Sviralom će svirati i tako začarati zmaja, jer je ljeskova mladica imala neku tajnu moć.

Uputivši se prema tvrđavi, čas se molio Bogu, čas svirao na sviralu. Kada je došao k tvrđavi, postavi se pokraj teških željeznih vrata, svirajući što je ljepše mogao. Tako je svirao tri dana. Treći dan, u jedanaest sati noću, teška vrata počeše škripati i pomalo se otvarati, te se na njima pomoli zmaj. Kada je izašao sva se zemlja tresla, nebo je potamnjelo i počelo je grmjeti. Ali pastiru to nije smetalo, već je još bolje svirao, jer je znao da zmaj voli slušati glazbu.

KING'S DAUGHTER

*T*here once lived a king who had a very beautiful daughter. Many young suitors who were princes came to see her, but she refused them all. She had her eyes on a handsome shepherd who played flute and sang beautifully. Every day the king's daughter went to the forest to see him.

One day she went to the shepherd and told him: "I am the king's daughter. My father wants me to marry a prince, but I am in love with you and wish to marry you. I came to see you today and ask if you will agree to it." Upon hearing this, the shepherd was frightened, gathered up all his sheep, and ran home.

Soon after, a foreign army overtook the kingdom. The king and his family were enslaved by the powerful army, and the young princess was locked in a high fortress, guarded by a dragon with seven heads. The enemy said that only one who was courageous enough to free the prisoner from the fortress would be able to marry her and inherit her kingdom. Many princes attempted to rescue the king's daughter, but they were all unsuccessful. The seven-headed dragon who guarded the tower killed everyone who attempted to save her.

The shepherd heard about the plight of the king's daughter and remembered that she had once told him she would marry him. So he decided to save her. Before he set out, he made a beautiful flute from the branch of a year-old hazel tree. He would play the flute and enchant the dragon, since the young hazel branch had magical power.

As the young shepherd made his journey toward the fortress, he was praying to God one moment and playing his flute the next. When he arrived at the fortress, he placed himself by the heavy iron doors.

Odjednom je zasvirao jednu lijepu pjesmicu koja je jako zanijela zmaja, te je slušao kao ošamućen. Pastir iskoristi tu prigodu i stade se korak po korak približavati vratima. Kada mu je uspjelo doći do njih, skoči unutra i zatvori teška vrata za sobom, te nastavi svirati. Vidjevši da je ostao vani, zmaj poče bučiti i tući repom po vratima tako jako da su se od udaraca tresla. Ali ući nije mogao. Ta je galama potrajala sve do trećih pjevanja pijetlova u zoru. Tada je zmaju prestala moć, a pastir se uputio dalje u dvorac, tražeći kraljevu kćer.

Trčeći od sobe do sobe napokon se nađe u sobi navrh kule. Čim ga je kraljevna opazila, lice joj se zažarilo, a pastir je skočio k njoj, veselo je zagrlio i upitao: "Lijepa kraljevno, hoćeš li se vjenčati sa mnom?" Kraljevna mu ovije ruke oko vrata i reče: "Već sam ti rekla da si moj!" Pastir uzme djevojku u naručje, iznese je iz tvrđave, s njom se vjenča i zagospodari kraljevstvom.

Thus he played the best he could for three days. On the third night, at half-past eleven, the heavy doors began to creak and slowly open, exposing the dragon. When he came out of the fortress, the whole earth shook, the sky darkened, and thunder echoed all around. But this did not trouble the shepherd. He played the flute even more beautifully, because he knew the dragon loved to listen to music. Suddenly he began to play a beautiful melody that enraptured the dragon who listened in a daze. The shepherd took advantage of the dragon's state and moved closer to the doors, step by step. When at last he managed to reach the entrance, he quickly jumped inside and closed the heavy doors behind him, continuing to play. Having been left outside, the dragon started to roar and beat at the doors with its tail with such force that they shook. But the dragon could not break through. The horrible sound continued until the third crow of the rooster at dawn. Then the dragon's power ceased, and the shepherd ventured further into the castle, looking for the king's daughter.

Searching room after room, he finally found her at the top of the tower. As soon as the princess saw him, her face became radiant, and the shepherd jumped happily to embrace her, asking: "Beautiful princess, will you marry me?" The princess put her arms around his neck and answered: "I already told you that you are mine!" The shepherd took the maiden into his arms and out of the fortress. He married her and ruled the kingdom.

King's Daughter, A Witch

Kraljeva Kći Vještica

Kraljeva kći
Vještica

Neki kralj imao kćer jedinicu. Ona bi svaki dan nove cipele dobivala. Kralj se već ljutio zbog toga što ona svaki dan jedne cipele podere.

Jednom mu padne na pamet kako će to saznati, pa razglasi po svemu kraljevstvu svome da će onome koji mu to otkrije dati pola kraljevstva i kćer za ženu. Svakakvi momci, carevi i kraljevi, kušali sreću, ali nisu ništa doznali. Jednoga dana dođe na dvor nekakav stari isluženi vojnik, pa se javi da će on doznati.

Oko pola dvanaest dođe kraljeva kći polako u kuhinju da vidi spava li vojnik. Vojnik se pretvara da spava, pa hrče. Djevojka, ne bi li se još bolje uvjerila, uzme svijeću pa mu brkove opali, a on ni da trepne, već spava. Tada ona izvuče iz njedara kamen, namaže njime potplate na cipelama, baci kamen i odleti kao munja kroz dimnjak. Kada je vojnik to vidio, namaže i on cipele, pa bjež' i on kroz dimnjak i dođe na lijepu ravnicu: djevojka u bijeg, a on za njom. Tako su se dugo vijali i najednom djevojka nestane, a on krenu ni lijevo, ni desno, već ravno naprijed.

Idući dugo dođe u šumu u kojoj su drveću grane i lišće od bakra, pa uzme jednu grančicu i metne je u torbu; onda dođe u šumu koja je bila srebrna, pa opet uzme jednu grančicu, a tako učini i u šumi od zlata.

Odjednom dođe na jednu ravnicu koja je bila od samog mramora i vidi gdje se dva vraga svađaju, te ih zapita: "Zašto se vi svađate?"

A oni mu odgovore: "Evo vidiš, imamo jedne opanke, a kada ih obuješ možeš jedinim korakom sedam milja prevaliti; zatim imamo ovaj šešir, s njim možeš po zraku letjeti, a ovu kabanicu kada obučeš, nitko te ne vidi, i još kada

KING'S DAUGHTER,
A WITCH

*T*here once lived a king with an only child, a daughter. Every day she needed a new pair of shoes. The king was angry because she would wear out the shoes within a day of receiving them.

One day he decided to find out what was going on, so he announced throughout the kingdom that the one who could find out what his daughter was doing with her shoes would be given half of his kingdom and his daughter as a bride. All kinds of youths, princes, and kings tried their luck, but no one could discover anything. One day an old, experienced soldier came to the castle and announced that he would investigate.

In the evening, at about half-past eleven, the king's daughter tiptoed into the kitchen to see whether the soldier was sleeping. The soldier pretended to be asleep and snored. The girl, to make certain, took a candle and burned a tip of his mustache. He made no response and still appeared to be asleep. Then she reached into her blouse and took out a stone, rubbed it against the soles of her shoes, threw it down, and flew up the chimney in a flash of lightning. When the soldier saw this, he rubbed his own shoes, and he also went through the chimney. He found himself in a beautiful field, the girl running ahead and he just behind. He followed her for a long time when suddenly the girl disappeared, and he turned neither left nor right but went straight ahead.

After continuing in this manner for quite some time, he came to a forest in which tree branches and leaves were made of copper, and he took one little branch and put it in his bag. Then he came to a silver forest, and there he also took a branch. He did the same in a golden forest.

se njome ogrneš, možeš biti tamo gdje si zamislio. Pa vidiš, mi bismo to rado među sobom podijelili ali ne znamo kako."

"E pa to je najlakše, već ću vas ja pomiriti, ali najprije da vidim je li to štogod vrijedno."

On obuče sve pa se brzo ogrne i zamisli da bude ondje gdje je kraljeva kći.

Kako se ogrnuo, tako se stvorio u jednom lijepom dvorcu gdje same vile plešu, pa među njima spazi i kraljevu kćer, a na ruci joj dijete. Vojnik dođe i sakrije se u svojoj kabanici pod stol, a nije ga nitko vidio. Najednom spusti djevojka dijete na zamlju pa ode plesati. Dijete dođe baš do stola pa se počne igrati zlatnom jabukom koju mu je kraljeva kći dala. Kako se igralo, ispadne mu jabuka iz ruke, a vojnik s njom u torbu. Dijete je počne tražiti, ali jabuke nema.

Kada je bilo pola jedan, svi krenu kući. Kraljeva kći također, a vojnik za njom. Kada je već blizu grada bio, ogrne se i zamisli da bude u kuhinji i da spava. I to se dogodi. Poslije njega dođe kraljeva kći kroz dimnjak u kuhinju i kada zapazi da vojnik spava, ode polako u svoju sobu.

Ujutro reče vojnik kralju da je saznao kako djevojka cipele podere, te mu ispripovjedi kako se sve dogodilo.

Kralj pozove odmah kćer te joj reče da ju je vojnik vidio kako je među vješticama plesala. No ona mu reče neka on to dokaže. Vojnik uzme svoju torbu i izvadi najprije bakrenu grančicu, onda srebrnu, a na kraju jabuku kojom se dijete igralo, pa je metne na stol. Djevojka tada sve prizna.

Kralj je dade tom vojniku za ženu i s njom pola svoga kraljevstva.

Next, he came to a plain, entirely made of marble, and he saw two devils there arguing, so he asked them: "Why are you arguing?"

They answered: "You see, we have a pair of shoes. Once you put them on, you can cross seven miles in one step; then we have this hat with which you can fly in the air; and this cloak – if you put it on, no one can see you. If you put it over your shoulders, you can be wherever you wish. We would like to divide this between us, but we do not know how."

"Well, that is simple. I will make peace between you, but let me see if this is worth anything."

He put everything on and threw the cloak over his shoulders and thought he would like to be wherever the king's daughter is.

As soon as he had put on the cloak, he found himself in a beautiful castle filled with dancing witches, and among them he noticed the king's daughter with a child in her arms. The soldier, wearing the cloak, came in and hid under a table. No one could see him. The girl then lowered the child to the floor and began dancing. The child came right up to the table and began playing with a golden apple from the king's daughter. As the child was playing, the apple rolled away. The soldier grabbed it and put it in his bag. The child began to look for the apple, but it was no longer there.

At half-past twelve, everyone went home. The king's daughter took her leave as well, and the soldier behind her. When they were nearing the city, the soldier put on the cloak and made a wish to be in the kitchen sleeping. Instantly he appeared there, and the king's daughter arrived through the chimney into the kitchen right after him. She noted that the soldier was asleep, and she quietly returned to her room.

In the morning the soldier told the king he knew how the daughter was wearing out her shoes, and he recounted everything that had happened.

Immediately, the king summoned his daughter and told her that the soldier had seen her dance among witches. But she refused to admit anything and insisted that the soldier provide some evidence. The soldier then took his bag and pulled out first a copper branch, then a silver one and, at the end, the

golden apple with which the child had been playing. He put it all on the table. Upon seeing the contents of the bag, the girl confessed to everything.

The king gave the soldier half of his kingdom and his daughter as a wife.

LITTLE FAIRY

MALA VILA

MALA VILA

*B*ili kralj i kraljica pa imali jedinca sina. Kad je kraljević već narastao, proslaviše njegovo šišano kumstvo i na čast pozvaše najviđenije ljude iz svoga kraljevstva. Bijeli dvori zasjaše od zlata, srebra i dragog kamenja i od tisuću svijeća. Kad uvečer u vrtu povedoše kolo, uhvatiše se djevojke sve jedna ljepša od druge, a sve gledahu u kraljevića milo i drago, da ga pojedu očima.

U ponoć se raziđoše gosti, a kraljević ode u gaj od starih lipa, jer je bila mjesečina kao dan a njemu se nije spavalo. Čarobno bješe pogledati na tamne sjene debeloga drveća. Kroz granje se uvlačila mjesečina i padala po zemlji u čudnim šarama. Lipe su mirisale kao tamjan iz crkve. Kraljević je polagano šetao, zamišljen, po mekanoj travici. Kad je izišao na proplanak, najednom ugleda pred sobom usred mjesečine na travi malu vilu odjevenu u krasne haljine od finog platna zlatom vezena. Kosa joj je bila duga i spuštena niz pleća, a na glavi joj se blistaše zlatna kruna ukrašena dragim kamenjem. Ali je bila posve, posve mala. Kao lučica!

Kraljević u čudu zastane i zagleda se u nju, a ona progovori glasom kao da srebrno zvonce zvoni: "Moj lijepi kraljeviću! I ja sam bila pozvana na tvoje kumovanje, ali nisam smjela doći u kolo jer sam tako malena: nego ti se ovdje klanjam, na ovoj sjajnoj mjesečini, koja je meni sunčev sjaj."

Kraljeviću se mala vila svidje. Nije se nimalo poplašio od ove noćne pojave, nego joj pristupi i uze je za ručicu. Ali mu se ona ote i nestade je. Ostade mu u ruci samo njena rukavica, tako mala da ju je jedva navukao na svoj najmanji prst. Tužan se vrati u dvore i nikome ne reče ni riječi s kim je bio.

Ali, drugu noć opet dođe u vrt. Hodio je po bijeloj mjesečini i tražio malu vilu. Ali, nje nigdje ne bješe. Od žalosti izvadi iz njedara malu rukavicu i

LITTLE FAIRY

*O*nce there lived a king and queen who had an only son. When the prince grew up, they celebrated his confirmation and, in honor, invited the most prominent people in the kingdom. The royal court was shining in gold, silver, and precious stones, and a thousand candles. When in the evening they began a dance in the garden, the young maidens joined hands in a circle, one prettier than the other, all looking dearly at the prince as if devouring him with their eyes.

At midnight, the guests dispersed and the prince went into the small forest by the old linden tree, because it was light as day in the moonlight, and he was not sleepy. It was magical to look at the dark shadows of huge trees. The moonlight pulled in through the branches and fell to the ground in unusual shades. The linden tree had a fragrance of incense from the church. The prince walked slowly, in thought, over soft grass. When he came out into the clearing, he suddenly saw in front of him in the moonlight on the grass a little fairy, dressed in a beautiful dress of fine cloth embroidered in gold. Her hair was long and went down her back, and on her head shone a golden crown decorated with precious stones. But she was very, very small; like a lightening bug!

The prince in wonder stopped and looked at her, as she uttered in a voice that sounded like the ring of a golden bell: "My beautiful prince! I also was invited to your confirmation, but was not allowed to join the circle for I am so small: here I bow to you, in this radiant moonlight, which for me is sunshine."

The prince was pleased with the little fairy. He was not at all frightened by this nightly appearance and approached her, taking her by the hand. But

poljubi je. U taj mah stvori se pred njim vila. Kraljević se toliko obradovao da se ne može iskazati koliko. Sve mu je srce u grudima igralo od miline. Dugo su šetali po mjesečini i čavrljali. Kraljević se začudi kad opazi da mala vila sve jednako raste dok s njim govori. Kad su se rastali, bila je dvaput veća nego sinoć. Kad joj je vratio rukavicu, nije je mogla više navući.

"Uzmi je, pa je čuvaj kao amanet," reče mala vila i nestade je.

"Nosit ću je na srcu," reče kraljević.

Svaku noć su se odsad sastajali njih dvoje u bašti. Dok je sunce sijalo, kraljević je muku mučio. Cio dan je bio tužan, jedva je čekao da izađe mjesec i samo je na nju mislio i pitao se hoće li noćaš doći.

Kraljević je sve više ljubio malu vilu, a ona je svaku noć rasla i bila sve veća i veća. Kad je prošlo devet noći, bješe pun mjesec, a vila je narasla velika kao kraljević. Veselo ga dočeka i reče: "Dokle god bude mjesečine, ja ću ti dolaziti."

"A ne, moja draga! Ja ne mogu živjeti bez tebe. Ti moraš biti sasvim moja. Ja ću te učiniti kraljicom."

"Dragi moj," reče vila, "hoću biti tvoja, ali samo tada ako ćeš me uvijek i samo mene jedinu voljeti."

"Uvijek, uvijek!" povikao je kraljević bez razmišljanja. "Samo tebe, druge nikad ni pogledat neću."

"Dobro! Ali pamti što kažem: samo dokle budeš držao riječ, bit ću tvoja."

Poslije tri dana proslaviše svadbu dvoje mladih. Ljepoti vilinoj se divio sav svijet.

Sretno su živjeli sedam godina i onda umrije stari kralj. Na sahranu mu dođoše mnogi podanici. Pored odra čuvale su mrtvaca najljepše gospođe iz čitave zemlje. Bila je ovdje i jedna djevojka crvene kose a crna oka. Ta se nije Bogu molila, nit je mrtvog kralja gledala, nego je samo očima pratila mladoga kraljevića. Vidio je i on da ga lijepa gospođa gleda i bilo mu drago. Kad je velika pogrebna povorka krenula na groblje, pogledao je kraljević tri puta u zamamnu ljepoticu, vodeći za ruku svoju ženu. Najednom mu se žena spotakne na svoju suknju i malo što ne pade.

she broke free and disappeared. In his hand remained only her glove, so small that he could hardly put it on his pinkie. He returned to the castle sad and told no one with whom he was.

But, the next night he again went to the garden. He walked in the white moonlight and looked for the little fairy. But she was nowhere. In sadness he pulled the little glove out of his chest and kissed it. In that moment the fairy appeared before him. The prince was so delighted, so much so that it cannot be described. In his chest his heart was pounding from delight. They walked for a long time in the moonlight and talked. The prince was surprised when he noticed that the little fairy was growing as she was talking with him. When they departed, she was twice the size she was the night before. When he returned her glove, she could no longer put it on.

"Take it and keep is as a pledge," said the little fairy and then she disappeared.

"I will carry it in my heart," said the prince.

Every night from then on the two of them met in the garden. While the sun shone, the prince grieved in agony. All day he was sad, he could hardly wait for the moon to come out, thought only about her, and wondered whether she would come at night.

The prince more and more loved the little fairy, and every night she grew and was bigger and bigger. When nine nights passed, it was a full moon, and the fairy was as big as the prince. Happily she waited for him and said: "As long as there is moonlight, I will come."

"Not so, my dear! I cannot live without you. You have to be mine. I will make you a queen."

"My dear," said the fairy. "I want to be yours, but only when you will love me, and only me, forever."

"Forever, forever!" shouted the prince without thinking. "Only you, I will never look at anyone else."

"Good! But remember when I say: as long as you hold on to your word, I will be yours."

"Jao! Gle, suknja mi je preduga!" uzviknu. Kraljević nije ni opazio da se ona smanjila.

Kad su sahranili staroga kralja, pođe ona ljepotica crvene kose odmah uz kraljevića putem kući, a on je ispod oka sve u nju pogledavao. Tako nije vidio da mu je žena sve manja. Kad stigoše kući pod stare lipe – nestade je posve.

Sada kraljević uzme za ženu gospođu crvene kose a crnih očiju. Ali s njome nije ni tri dana sretno živio. Tražila je da joj kupi postelju od samog dragog kamena, željela je sad ovo, sad ono, a sve same stvari kakvih i nema na svijetu. Kad on nije mogao da joj ispuni želje, ona je plakala, svađala se s njim, grdila ga. Kad mu bješe već dozlogrdilo, on je otjera.

Sad tek vidje što je učinio. Uzdisao je i jadikovao za malom vilom. Ponovo je odlazio pod stare lipe svake noći obasjane mjesečinom da dozove svoju lijepu i dobru vilu. Zvao je i zvao, čekao i čekao, i već postao i starac.

Ali se ona nikada više nije vratila.

Three days later they celebrated the wedding of the two youths. The whole world admired the fairy's beauty.

They lived happily for seven years and then the old king died. Many citizens came to the funeral. At the bier, the casket was guarded by the most beautiful women in the whole country. Present was a maiden with red hair and dark eyes. She did not pray to God, nor did she look at the dead king, but only followed the prince with her eyes. He also saw the beautiful woman look at him and was pleased. When the large funeral procession moved to the cemetery, the prince looked three times at the tempting beauty, while holding his wife by hand. Suddenly his wife tripped on her skirt and almost fell.

"Oh! Look, my skirt is too long!" she shouted. The prince did not even notice that she was becoming smaller.

When they buried the old king, the beauty with the red hair immediately followed the prince on the way home, and he continued looking at her under his eye. Thus, he did not see that his wife was getting smaller and smaller. When they arrived home, she disappeared under the old linden tree.

Now the prince took the woman with red hair for his wife. But he did not live happily with her even for three days. She wanted him to buy her bedding out of diamonds, she wanted now this, now that, things that did not exist in this world. When he could not fulfill her wishes, she cried, quarreled with him, and scolded him. When he could no longer take it, he drove her away.

Only then did he realize what he did. He sighed and lamented for his little fairy. Again, every night, he went under the old linden tree illuminated by the moonlight, calling to his beautiful and good fairy. He called and called, waited and waited, and even became an old man.

But she never came back again.

Little Frog Maiden

Žabica Djevojka

ŽABICA DJEVOJKA

Živjeli jednom muž i žena i već su bili gotovo ostarjeli, a djeteta nisu imali. Uvijek su Boga molili da im dade kakvo dijete. Pođu naposljetku na jedno proštenje i opet zamole Boga da im dade dijete, pa makar bila i žabica.

Vrate se natrag kući i zaista, žena osjeti da je zanijela i za devet mjeseci rodi ona, ali što? Žabicu! Ali i s time su bili veseliji nego bez ičega. Žabica je bila uvijek vani u vinogradu i rijetko kada je kući dolazila. Muž je uvijek radio u vinogradu, a žena mu svaki dan nosila objed. Ali kako je već bila ostarjela, počela se jednoga dana žaliti kako se više ne može pokrenuti, a kamoli mužu ići s objedom, jer joj noge više ništa ne valjaju. Tada dođe izvana kći žabica, a imala je već četrnaest godina, pa reče: "Majko! Vidim da ste stari, da više ne možete hodati, niti ići ocu s objedom, već dajte objed, idem ja s njim."

"Draga moja kćeri žabice, kako bi ti išla s objedom kada ga nećeš moći ni nositi, pa nemaš ni ruke kojima bi uhvatila lonac."

"Moći ću nositi," govori žabica. "Stavite mi lonac na leđa i vežite mi ga za noge, pa se ne bojte."

"E pa probaj, ako budeš mogla."

Stavi joj lonac na leđa, veže joj ga za noge i pošalje je ocu. Žabica nosila, nosila, a kada je došla do ograde vrta gdje joj je bio otac, nije ju mogla otvoriti ni preskočiti, pa poče oca zvati. Otac dođe, uzme s nje lonac i počne jesti. Žabica mu tad reče neka je digne na jednu trešnju. Kada ju je digao, ona počne pjevati. Pjevala je da je sve odzvanjalo i to tako lijepo, rekao bi čovjek da to vile pjevaju.

Prolazio je tuda kraljev sin, koji je bio došao u lov i začuo pjesmu. Kada je pjesma utihnula, priđe starcu i upita ga tko to tako lijepo pjeva. Starac reče da ne zna, jer nikoga niti vidi niti čuje, osim gavrana što nad njim lete.

LIttle FROg MAIDEN

*T*here once lived an old man and his wife who did not have any children. They continuously prayed to God for a child. On one occasion they went to a religious feast and asked God to give them a child, even if it were but a little frog.

They returned home and the wife noticed she had conceived. In nine months she gave birth, but to what? A little frog! And they were happy even with this than with nothing. The little frog was always outside in the vineyard, and rarely did she come into the house. The husband always worked in the vineyard, and the wife brought him lunch every day. But as she was already getting old, one day she began to complain about how she could hardly move, let alone bring lunch to her husband. Her feet were no longer as good as before.

Just then the daughter, a little frog who was already fourteen, came into the house and said: "Mother! I see that you are old and can no longer walk to give father his lunch. Give me the lunch and I will take it to him."

"My dear little frog daughter, how will you deliver the lunch when you cannot even carry it? You don't have hands with which to carry the pot."

"I can carry it," said the little frog. "Put the pot on my back and tie it to my legs. Don't worry."

"Well, go ahead and try, if you are able."

Mother put the pot on the frog's back, tied it to her legs, and sent her off to father. The little frog carried and carried the pot. When she arrived at the fence of the yard where father was working, she couldn't open it or jump over it, so she called out to him. Father came, took the pot and began to eat. The little frog asked him to lift her and place her on a cherry tree, and once she

"Ma ipak mi recite, tko god da je; ako je muškarac bit će moj drug, ako je djevojka bit će moja draga."

Ali starca je bilo i sram i strah, pa reče da ne zna. Kraljev sin ode kući.

Drugi dan donese opet žabica starom ocu objed i opet je on diže na trešnju, i ona počne pjevati, i gle, dođe kraljev sin namjerno tamo u lov kako bi opet čuo pjesmu i vidio tko pjeva. Žabica pjeva sa trešnje da sva dolina odjekuje. Kada je pjesma prestala, priđe kraljev sin starcu, pa ga pita tko to pjeva. Starac mu reče da ne zna.

"A tko ti je objed donio?" pita ga kraljev sin.

"Ja sam," veli starac, "sâm kući išao, pa sam bio umoran, tako da nisam mogao jesti te sam ga sa sobom donio."

"Ta me pjesma dira u srce, vi starče sigurno znate tko pjeva, recite mi; ako je muškarac bit će mi drug, ako je djevojka bit će moja draga."

Sada starac odgovori: "Ja bih vam rekao, ali me je sram, a vi biste se i ljutili."

"Ma ne bojte se, već mi recite."

On mu tada ispriča da to žabica pjeva i da je to njegova kći.

"Recite joj neka siđe dolje."

Žabica siđe i još jedanput zapjeva. Mladiću srce poskoči od veselja, pa joj reče: "Budi moja draga. Sutra će doći djevojke moje dvojice braće i koja od njih donese najljepši cvijet, kralj će njoj i njezinom zaručniku dati kraljevstvo. Za moju dragu dođi ti i tamo ponesi cvijet kakav odabereš."

Žabica mu kaže: "Doći ću kao što želiš, ali ti trebaš iz dvorca poslati bijeloga pijetla na kojem ću dojahati."

On ode i pošalje joj bijeloga pijetla. Ona pak ode k Suncu i zamoli sunčane haljine. Sutradan ujutro, zajaše žabica pijetla, a sunčane haljine uzme sa sobom. Kada je takva došla do gradske straže, nisu je htjeli pustiti. No kada reče da će ih tužiti kraljevu sinu ako je ne puste, pustiše je. Čim je ušla u grad pijetao se pretvori u bijelu vilu, a žabica u najljepšu djevojku na svijetu.

Odjene sunčane haljine, a kao cvijet ponese klas pšenice i tako dođe u kraljevu palaču.

was perched there she began to sing. Her voice resounded so enchantingly one might have imagined the fairies were singing.

One day it happened that the king's son had been hunting in the area, and as he passed by, he heard the beautiful voice. When the singing stopped, he came up to the old man and asked him who had been singing so well. The old man claimed that he didn't know because he could neither see nor hear anyone except the gulls flying overhead.

"But tell me who you think it might be. If it is a man, he will be my friend. If it is a maiden, she will be my dear one."

The old man was ashamed and afraid, so he claimed not to know. The king's son returned home.

The next day the little frog again brought her father lunch, and again he lifted her onto a branch of the cherry tree. She began singing and, alas, the king's son was there already. The king had come specifically to that place to hunt and to find out who was singing. The little frog sang so well from her perch in the cherry tree that the whole valley resonated. When the song had finished, the king's son approached the old man, requesting again to know who was singing. The old man still claimed not to know.

"And who brought you lunch?" the king's son inquired.

"I did," the old man said. "I went home and was too tired to eat, so I brought the lunch back with me."

"That song touches my heart, old man. You surely know who is singing. Tell me. If it is a man, he will be my friend. If it is a maiden, she will be my dear one."

This time the old man replied: "I would tell you, but I am ashamed and you will probably be angry."

"Don't be afraid but do tell me who is singing this beautiful song."

The old man finally told him it was his daughter, the little frog, who was singing.

"Tell her to come down."

Kralj priđe dragoj najstarijega sina i upita je kakav je cvijet donijela. Ona mu pokaže ružu. Dođe do drage srednjega sina pa upita kakav je ona cvijet donijela. Ona mu pokaže karanfil. Okrene se k dragoj najmlađega sina, opazi kod nje klas pšenice, pa joj reče: "Ti si nam najbolji i najkorisniji cvijet donijela; vidi se da znaš kako se bez pšenice ne da živjeti i da ćeš znati gospodariti. Što će nam drugo cvijeće i oholost? Udaj se za mog najmlađeg sina kojemu si draga, i njemu ću ostaviti svoje kraljevstvo."

I tako je žabica postala kraljica.

The little frog came down and sang the song once more. The young man's heart leapt with joy, and he said to her: "Be my dear one. Tomorrow my brothers' maidens will come, and the one who brings the most beautiful flower will receive, with her betrothed, the kingdom from the king. You can come as my maiden and bring a flower of your choice."

The little frog answered him: "I will come as you wish, but you will have to send a white rooster from the castle upon which I will arrive."

The young man left and immediately sent her a white rooster. She went and asked the Sun for a sunlit dress. The next morning the little frog rode upon the rooster and carried with her the sunlit dress. When she arrived at the city gate, the guards detained her, unwilling to let her in. She told them she would report this to the king's son. They consented at last, and she was allowed to pass through the gate. As soon as she entered the city, the rooster changed into a white fairy, and the little frog became the most beautiful maiden in the whole world.

She wore the sunlit dress and chose a sheaf of wheat as the flower, and she made her appearance at the king's palace.

First the king approached the oldest son's maiden, asking what flower she had brought. She showed him a rose. He then approached the middle son's maiden, asking what flower she had brought. She showed him a carnation. He turned to the youngest son's maiden, noticing she had a sheaf of wheat, and he said to her: "You brought us the best and most useful flower. I can see you know one cannot live without wheat, and you will know how to manage. Of what use are other flowers and pride? Marry my youngest son who loves you and to whom I will leave my kingdom."

And thus the little frog became a queen.

Rosemary Bush

Busen Ružmarina

BUSEN RUŽMARINA

*B*ili čovjek i žena, a djeteta nisu imali. Jednom u šetnji našli busen ružmarina kako cvate i žena reče: "Bože moj, evo i ružmarin cvate i plodove ima, samo ja nemam. Da mi Bog dâ da imam makar busen ružmarina."

I zanijela je. Rodi busen ružmarina, posadi ga u teglu i stavi na prozor. Svaki dan ga je lijepo pazila i zalijevala.

Nasuprot njihovoj kući bio je kraljev dvorac. Jednoga dana dođe k njoj kralj i zamoli je da mu proda taj busen ružmarina. A ona mu reče da ne može, jer je to njezin porod. Kralj joj je nudio zlata koliko god želi, jer grm je bio pred njegovim dvorcem i vidio je da iz grma svaki dan izlazi lijepa djevojčica. Ponovno je molio i obećao da će grm staviti nasuprot njezinoj kući kako bi ga i ona mogla svaki dan gledati. Ona pristane.

Kralj je učinio kako je obećao i svaki je dan ružmarin lijepo zalijevao. Djevojčica iz ružmarina svaki je dan dolazila pospremiti mu sobu, ali je nikako nije mogao uhvatiti. Jednog dana uđe u sobu i legne u krevet kao da spava. Djevojčica uđe i počne spremati, a on je uhvati i reče joj: "Ostani, nemoj više ići u cvijet, već budi moja."

A ona mu odgovori: "Ne mogu, moram ostati u cvijetu dvadeset godina, tek tada mogu izaći."

On upita: "Kako bih mogao svaki dan kada dođem kući s tobom porazgovarati?"

Ona mu dade jedno zvonce i reče mu: "Kada zazvoniš, ja ću doći, ali ovo zvonce uvijek čuvaj uza se."

Tako su radili dugo vremena. Jednoga dana on je trebao otići na dalek put i u brzini na stoliću zaboravio zvonce.

Prije polaska slugama je naredio da ne zalijevaju cvijet toplom vodom.

ROSEMARY BUSH

*T*here once lived a man and wife who wanted a family but had no children. One day while taking a walk, they came across a rosemary bush in bloom. The wife said: "My Lord, here is a rosemary bush covered with blossoms, but I myself cannot flower. If only God were to give me even a rosemary bush."

Not long after, she discovered that she was pregnant. A rosemary bush was born! She planted it in a pot and placed it on the windowsill, where she watched and watered it every day.

Across from the man and wife's house was the king's palace. One day the king came to visit and asked the woman to give him the rosemary bush. She told him that she could not, for she had given birth to it herself. Because the rosemary bush was right in view of his castle, every day he could see a little girl leap out of the plant. The king offered the woman as much gold as she wished, but she refused to give him the rosemary bush. The king asked again, promising to keep the bush right in front of his castle, so she too would be able to look upon it daily. She agreed.

The king upheld his promise and watered the rosemary bush every day. The girl would leap out of the plant and come to tidy his room, but he could never catch her. One day he came to his room and went to bed as if to sleep. When the girl appeared and began to clean, he caught her and said: "Stay, do not return to the flower, and be mine."

She replied: "I cannot. I will remain in the rosemary bush for twenty years. Only then can I come out."

He asked her: "How can I speak to you every day when I come here?"

She gave him a bell and said: "When you ring, I will come, but keep this bell near you always."

Zvonce je zaboravio. Kada su sluge pospremale, zvonce se prevrne i zazvoni, a djevojčica dođe. I oni je izudaraju tako da je bila sva modra, jedva se u cvijet vratila.

Po povratku kralj vidje da mu je cvijet počeo venuti. Upita sluge zašto cvijet vene, što su mu učinili, jesu li ga zalijevali toplom vodom. Oni zaniječu. I tada on stade zvoniti – zvoni, zvoni, nikoga nema. Dugo je zvonio, kad najednom, evo je, jedva se izvukla, jedva ide k njemu i reče mu: "Jesam li ti rekla da zvonce ne ostavljaš?"

A on joj reče: "A što ti je?"

"Sluge su zvonile, ja sam došla, a oni me namlatili da sam sva modra."

On je upita čime bi je liječio.

Ona mu reče: "Samo čistom vodom me svaki dan polijevaj, a jednom na dan vodom od ružmarina."

Tako ju je izliječio i kada je navršila dvadeset godina izišla je iz ružmarina. Kralj ju je oženio, a ona je k sebi pozvala majku i oca.

They continued visiting this way for a long time.

One day the king had to go on a long journey, and in his haste he forgot the bell, leaving it on a little table. Before departure he told his servants not to water the flower with warm water. When the servants were cleaning, the bell slipped off the table. It rang, causing the girl to appear. They beat her so hard she was bruised blue, and she could barely return to the bush.

Upon his return, the king noticed that the flower was wilting. He asked his servants why it was wilting and what they had done to it. Had they watered it with warm water? He began to ring the bell. He rang and rang, but no one came. He continued to ring for a long time, when at last she emerged, barely able to climb out of the flower. She walked toward him and said: "Didn't I tell you not to leave the bell?"

He asked her: "What has happened to you?"

"The servants rang, and I came, and they beat me; now I am all blue."

He asked how he could save her, and she told him: "Water me every day with clean water and once a day with rosemary water."

The king did as she asked. And when she turned twenty, she came out of the rosemary bush. The king married her, and she invited her mother and father to live with her in the castle.

Stribor's Forest

Šuma Striborova

ŠUMA STRIBOROVA

1.

Zašao neki momak u šumu Striborovu, a nije znao da je ono šuma začarana i da se u njoj svakojaka čuda zbivaju. Zbivala se u njoj čuda dobra, ali i naopaka – svakome po zasluzi.

Morala je pak ta šuma ostati začarana dokle god u nju ne stupi onaj kojemu je milija njegova nevolja nego sva sreća ovoga svijeta.

Nasjekao dakle onaj momak drva i sjeo na panj da počine, jer bijaše lijep zimski dan. Ali iz panja iziđe pred njega zmija i stade se umiljavati oko njega. Ono pak ne bijaše prava zmija nego bijaše ljudska duša, radi grijeha i zlobe ukleta, a mogao ju je osloboditi samo onaj koji bi se s njom vjenčao. Bljeskala se zmija kao srebro na suncu i gledala momku upravo u oči.

"Lijepe li gujice, Bože moj! Gotovo da bih je i kući ponio," progovori momak od šale.

"Evo budalaste glave koja će me osloboditi na svoju nesreću," pomisli grešna duša u guji, požuri se i pretvori se odmah od guje u ljepotu djevojku te stade pred momka. Rukavci joj bijeli i vézeni kao krila leptirova, a sitne nožice kao u banice. Ali kako bijaše zlobno pomislila, onako joj ostade u ustima gujin jezik.

"Evo me! Vodi me kući i vjenčaj se sa mnom!" reče guja-djevojka momku.

Sad da je ono bio siguran i dosjetljiv momak pa da je brže mahnuo ušicom od sjekire na nju i da je viknuo: "Nisam baš ja mislio da se sa šumskim čudom vjenčam," postala bi djevojka opet gujom, i utekla bi u panj i nikomu ništa.

STRIBOR'S FOREST

1.

One day a young man entered Stribor's forest, but he did not know that the forest was enchanted and that, in it, all kinds of miracles could occur. In the forest, there were good fortunes and bad ones – granted to each according to one's merit. The forest would remain enchanted until the day when someone would enter it whose own misfortune was dearer than all the happiness of this world.

The young man cut up the wood and sat on a tree stump to rest in the middle of a beautiful winter day. Out of the stump came a snake that began to flaunt herself to the young man. It wasn't a real snake but a human soul under a spell because of sin and evil. It could be freed only by the one who would marry it. The snake glittered like silver under the sun and looked the young man straight in the eye.

"What a pretty viper, my God! I would take it home," said the young man in jest.

"Here is a fool who will free me at his own unhappiness," thought the sinful soul in the viper. It hurriedly changed from a viper into a beautiful maiden and stood before the young man. Her sleeves were white and sewn like the wings of a butterfly, and her feet were tiny as those of the governor's wife. However, because she had an evil thought, the tongue of the viper remained in her mouth.

"Here I am! Take me home and marry me!" said the viper-girl to the young man.

Ali ono je bio neki dobričina, plašljiv i stidljiv mladić, pak ga bilo stid da joj ne ispuni želju kad se već radi njega pretvorila. A baš mu se i svidjela jer je bila ljepolika, a on, neuputan, nije mogao znati što joj je ostalo u ustima. Uze on djevojku za ruku i povede je kući. A živio je taj momak sa svojom starom majkom i pazio majku kao ikonu.

"Evo, majko, snahe," reče momak kad stigoše on i djevojka kući.

"Hvala Bogu, sinko," odvrati majka i pogleda ljepotu djevojku. Ali je majka bila stara i mudra i odmah spozna što imade snaha u ustima. Ode snaha da se preobuče, a mati reče sinu:

"Lijepu si mladu izabrao, samo pazi, sine, nije li ono guja!"

Sin se malone skamenio od čuda: otkud njegova mati znade da je ono bila guja? Razljuti se u srcu i pomisli: "Moja majka mora da je vještica." I odmah zamrzi na majku.

Počelo njih troje živjeti zajedno, ali ono zlo i naopako. Snaha jezičljiva, nazlobna, proždrljiva i goropadna.

Bila je tamo litica visoka do oblaka, pa snaha zapovjedi jednog dana starici neka joj donese snijega sa vrha litice da se umije.

"Nema puta na ovu visinu," reče starica.

"Uzmi kozu, neka te vodi. Kuda ona gore, tuda ti naglavce dolje," reče snaha.

Tamo bio i sin, pa se nasmijao na te riječi samo da ugodi svojoj ženi.

To se tako ražalilo majci da odmah pođe na liticu po snijeg, jer joj nije bilo žao života. Idući putem, htjela se pomoliti Bogu za pomoć, ali se predomisli govoreći: "Opazio bi Bog da mi sin ne valja."

No Bog joj ipak osta na pomoći, i ona sretno donese snahi snijega s litice ispod oblaka.

Drugog dana zapovjedi snaha baki: "Idi tamo na jezero zamrznuto. Usred jezera ima rupa. Uhvati mi na rupi šarana za ručak."

"Provalit će se led poda mnom, propast ću u jezero," odvrati baka.

"Radovat će se šaran, propadneš li s njime," reče snaha.

I opet se sin nasmijao, a baka se tako ražalostila da odmah ode na jezero.

Now, if he had been a smart and confident young man he would have swung at her with the blunt edge of his axe and shouted: "I do not have in mind to marry a forest wonder," and the girl would have immediately turned into a viper and disappeared under the stump, and that would be that.

But because he was kindhearted, fearful, and shy, he was ashamed not to fulfill her wish when she transformed for him. And she appealed to him because she was pretty, yet he, uninformed, did not know that part of the snake remained in her mouth. So, he took the girl by the hand and brought her home, where he lived with his old mother whom he worshipped as if she were a religious icon.

"Here is a daughter-in-law, Mother," said the young man when he returned home with the girl.

"Thank God, son!" replied his mother before she turned and looked at the pretty girl. The mother was old and wise and immediately became aware of what the daughter-in-law had in her mouth. When the daughter-in-law went to change, the mother said to her son: "You selected a pretty maiden but be cautious, son, this maiden may be a viper!"

The son was shocked and greatly dismayed. How could his mother know that this maiden indeed was a viper? Anger took over his heart and he thought: "My mother must be a witch." Immediately he began to hate his mother.

The three of them began to live together, but not happily. The daughter-in-law was talkative, malicious, greedy, and fierce.

Near the house there was a steep mountain as high as the sky, so the daughter-in-law one day ordered the old woman to bring her some snow from the top of the mountain to wash her face.

"There is no path there up the hill," said the old woman.

"Take a goat to show you the way. Wherever she goes up, you can tumble down," said the daughter-in-law.

The son was present and smiled at these words, just to please his wife.

Pucketa led pod bakom, plače ona da joj se suze po licu mrznu. Ali još neće da se Bogu moli, taji pred Bogom da joj je sin grešan.

"I bolje da poginem," misli baka i ide po ledu.

Ali još nije došlo vrijeme da baka umre. Zato preletje nad njom galeb, noseći ribu. Omakne se riba galebu i padne upravo pred baku. Baka uze ribu i donese sretno snasi.

Trećeg dana sjela baka uz ognjište i uzela sinovu košulju da je okrpa. Kad to vidje snaha, poletje do nje, istrže joj košulju iz ruku i viknu: "Ostavi to, sljepice stara, nisu to tvoji poslovi!"

I ne dade majci da okrpa sinovu košulju.

Sad se starici posve rastuži srce, te ona ode pred kuću, sjedne na onoj ciči zimi na klupu i pomoli se Bogu: "Bože moj, pomozi mi!"

Uto vidje ona kako k njoj ide neko ubogo djevojče, na njemu samo izderana rubina, a rame pomodrelo od studeni jer joj se rukav iskinuo. Ali se svejedno djevojče nasmijava jer je umilne ćudi. Pod pazuhom joj svežanj triješća.

"Hoćete li, bako, kupiti luči?" upita djevojče.

"Nemam novaca, kćerce, nego ako hoćeš da ti okrpam taj rukavčić," reče tužna baka koja je još držala u rukama iglu i konac za sinovu košulju.

Baka okrpa djevojčici rukav, a djevojka joj dade svežanj luči, zahvali joj milo i ode dalje, radosna što joj rame ne zebe.

The mother was so sad. She went up the mountain to find the snow, because she did not care about whether she died trying to find it. As she went up the mountain, she wanted to pray to God for help, but she changed her mind and said: "God will notice that my son is not good."

But God helped her anyway, and she safely brought snow from the high ridge to the daughter-in-law.

The next day the daughter-in-law ordered the old woman: "Go to the frozen lake. In the middle of the lake is a hole. Catch a carp for my lunch."

"The ice will break under me, and I will fall into the lake," replied the old woman.

"The carp will be happy if you fall in with it," said the daughter-in-law.

Again, the son laughed, and the old mother was so saddened that she immediately went to the lake. The ice cracked under her feet. As she cried, the tears froze on her face. But she still did not pray to God for help, trying to conceal from God that her son was sinful.

"It is better that I die," thought the old woman, as she continued on the ice.

But the time had not come for her to die. Just then a seagull flew above her, carrying a fish in its beak. The fish wriggled out of its beak and fell right in front of the old woman. The old woman took the fish and safely brought it back to her daughter-in-law.

On the third day the old woman sat by the fire and began to mend the son's shirt. When the daughter-in-law saw what she was doing, she flew to her and grabbed the shirt from her hands, yelling: "Leave this alone, blind old woman. This is not for you to do!"

And she did not allow the mother to mend her son's shirt.

Now the old woman's heart was completely broken, and she went out in front of the house and sat on the bench in the cold winter air. She prayed to God: "Dear God, help me!"

Just then she saw a poor young girl walking nearby, dressed in rags, her shoulders blue from the cold because her sleeve was torn. But the young girl

was smiling, showing her good nature. Under her arm she carried a bundle of twigs.

"Would you like to buy some twigs, Grandma?" asked the girl.

"I don't have any money, daughter, but if you want I can mend your sleeve," said the sad old woman, still holding the needle in her hand intended for her son's shirt.

The old woman mended the girl's sleeve, and the girl gave her in return a bundle of twigs, thanked her, and continued on her way, happy that her shoulder was no longer cold.

2.

*U*veče reče snaha baki: "Mi ćemo poći u goste kumi, a ti da si ugrijala vode dok se vratim."

Bila snaha proždrljiva i uvijek gledala gdje da se ugosti. Kad oni odoše, osta baka sama, pa uze onog triješća što joj ga prodalo djevojče, i potpali oganj na ognjištu, a onda ode u komoru po drva.

Dok je ona u komori tražila drva, začuje kako u kuhinji nešto pucka, nešto kucka: kuc! kuc!

"Tko je Božji?" upita baka iz komore.

"Domaći! Domaći!" ozovu se iz kuhinje neki sitni glasovi kao da žvrgolje vrapci pod strehom.

Dalo se baki na čudo što je ovo ovako u noći, i ona uđe u kuhinju. Kad ona tamo, ali ono se na ognjištu istom rasplamsale luči, a oko plamena zaigrali kolo "Domaći," sve sami mužići od jedva pô lakta. Na njima kožusi, kapice i opančići crveni kao plamenovi, kosa i brada sivi kao pepeo, a oči žarke kao živi ugljen.

Izlazi njih sve više i više iz plamena, svaka luč po jednog daje. Kako izlaze, tako se smiju i vrište, prebacuju se po ognjištu, cikću od veselja i hvataju se u kolo.

Pa zaigra kolo: po ognjištu, po pepelu, pod policu, na stolicu, po ćupu, na klupu! Igraj! Igraj! Brzo! Brže! Cikću, vrište, guraju se i krevelje. Sol prosuše, kvas proliše, brašno rastepoše! – sve od velike radosti. Vatra na ognjištu plamsa i sjaji, pucka i grije; a baka gleda i gleda. Nije joj žao ni soli ni kvasca, nego se raduje veselju što joj ga Bog šalje na utjehu.

Čini se baki da se pomladila – nasmije se kao grlica, poskoći kao curica, hvata se u kolo sa Domaćima pa zaigra. Ali joj ipak ostalo još čemera u srcu, a to bijaše tako teško te kolo odmah stade.

"Božja braćo," reče onda baka Domaćima, "biste li vi meni znali pomoći da ugledam jezik svoje snahe, pa kad kažem momu sinu što sam

2.

*I*n the evening, the daughter-in-law said to the old woman: "We are leaving to visit my godmother and, in the meantime, you must warm up some water."

The daughter-in-law was greedy and always looked for someone to visit. When they left, the old woman stayed and took the twigs that the poor girl had given her. She lit the fire on the hearth, and went to the shed to get some wood.

While she was looking for the wood, she heard something in the kitchen crackle, and pop. Pop! Pop!

"Who is it, by God!" asked the old woman from the other room.

"Domachi! Domachi!" came the reply from the kitchen, in tiny voices, as if sparrows were chirping under the eaves.

"What marvel is this in the night?" thought the old woman, as she entered the kitchen. Just as she entered, flames flared on the hearth like a torch, and around the flames Domachi danced in a circle, all little men hardly half an arm in length. They were dressed in fur coats; caps and soft-soled footwear, red like the flames; hair and beard, gray like ashes; and their eyes glowing like burning hot coals.

There were more of them coming out of the flames, one appearing out of each torch. And as they appeared, they laughed and shouted, jumped over the fire, shouted with joy, and joined in a circle.

They began to do a dance on the hearth, in the ashes, under the shelf, on the chair, in the jug, and on the bench! "Around and around! Faster and faster!" There was screaming, shouting, pushing, and making faces. They scattered the salt, the yeast, wasted the flour, all with great zeal. The fire on the hearth blazed, shined, crackled, and glowed. The old woman stared in amazement. She was not sorry for the salt or the yeast, but simply pleased with the joy God had sent to comfort her.

na svoje oči vidjela, možda se opameti?"

Baka stane pripovijedati Domaćima sve kako je bilo. Domaći posjedali uokolo po rubu ognjišta, nožice ovjesili niz ognjište, nanizali se kao čičak do čička i slušaju baku, pa sve klimaju glavom od čuda. Kako klimaju glavom, onako im se žare crvene kapice: mislio bi tko ono sama vatra na ognjištu plaminja.

Kad je baka svršila pripovijedanje, viknu jedan od Domaćih, po imenu Malik Tintilinić:

"Ja ću ti pomoći! Idem u sunčanu zemlju i donijet ću ti svračjih jaja. Podmetnut ćemo ih pod kokoš, pa kad se izlegu svračići, prevarit će se snaha: polakomit će se kao svaka šumska guja za svračićima i isplazit će jezik.

Svi Domaći ciknuše od radosti što se Malik Tintilinić tako dobro dosjetio. Još oni najbolje vrište, ali ide snaha iz gostiju i nosi sebi kolač.

Nasrne snaha ljutito na vrata da vidi tko to u kuhinji vrišti. Ali kad ona raskrili vrata, a ono: top! - prasne plamen, skočiše Domaći, topnuše svi u jedan mah nožicama o ognjište, ponesoše se nad plamen, poletješe pod krov – kvrcnuše daščice na krovu i nestade Domaćih.

Samo Malik Tintilinić ne uteče nego se sakrije u pepelu.

Kako je plamen iznenada prsnuo uvis, a vrata udarila o vratnicu, onako se uplašila snaha i od straha sjela na zemlju kao vreća. Rastepe joj se kolač po rukama, raspadnu joj se kose i češljevi, bulji oči i viče od jada: "Što je ovo bilo, nesreć stara?"

"Vjetar podigao plamen kad si otvorila vrata," reče baka i mudro se drži.

"A što je ono u pepelu?" opet će snaha, jer je iz pepela virila crvena peta opančića Malika Tintilinića.

"Ono je žeravica," odvraća baka.

Ali snaha ne vjeruje nego ustane onako raspletena i ide da vidi izbližega što je na ognjištu. Prikučila se licem do pepela, ali se Malik Tintilinić hitro baci nožicom i kvrcne petom snahu po nosu. Viče snaha kao da se u moru topi, sva je garava po licu, a pepeo joj posuo raščupane kose.

"Što je ovo, nesreć stara?" upita snaha.

She felt she had become younger – she smiled like a turtle dove, jumped up like a maiden, and joined the Domachi in their circle and danced. Yet, her heart ached, and it became so heavy that she stopped dancing.

"Dear God's brothers," said the old woman to the Domachi, "would you be able to help me see my daughter-in-law's tongue, so that when I tell my son what I saw myself, he might become smarter?"

The old woman began to tell the Domachi everything that had happened. The Domachi sat around the edge of the hearth, their little feet hanging over the hearth, one next to the other, like one burr next to another, listening to the old woman and shaking their heads in amazement. As they shook their heads, their red caps glowed.

When the old woman finished her story, one of the Domachi, by the name of Malik Tintilinich, shouted: "I will help you! I will go to the land of sunshine, and I will bring you magpie eggs. We will put them under the hen, and when the magpies are hatched, your daughter-in-law will betray herself. She will crave magpies as any forest viper and will put out her tongue."

All the Domachi twittered with joy that Malik Tintilinich had thought of something so good. They were still shouting when the daughter-in-law was returning from her visit carrying a cake for herself.

She rushed to the door to see who was making noise in the kitchen. But, as she opened the door with a bang, the flames flared up and all the Domachi jumped at once feet-first into the hearth, over the flames and up onto the roof. The boards in the roof creaked and the Domachi disappeared.

Only Malik Tintilinich didn't run but hid in the ashes.

As sparks suddenly rushed upwards, the door swung open and slammed against the doorpost, frightening the daughter-in-law who then flew in and landed on the floor in a heap. The cake that she had been carrying ended up in pieces all over her hands, and her hair had fallen down with the combs scattered on the floor. Her eyes were piercing as she shouted: "What was all of this, you old misfortune!"

"The wind blew up the flames when you opened the door," said the old woman, calmly.

"And what's in the ashes?" the daughter-in-law asked again, because a red heel of Malik Tintilinich's shoe was sticking out.

"That's live coal burning," replied the old woman.

But the daughter-in-law did not believe her and got up, still disheveled, to closely inspect the hearth. She put her face up to the ashes, just as little Malik Tintilinich quickly lifted his foot and kicked the daughter-in-law's nose. The daughter-in-law yelled as if she were calling for help; her face turned red, and ashes filled her tumbled hair.

"What is this, you old misfortune?" demanded the daughter-in-law.

"Live coal bursting with fire spattered all over you," replied the old woman, while Malik Tintilinich in the ashes burst out with laughter.

When the daughter-in-law stalked off to wash her face, the old woman showed Malik Tintilinich where in the small room the daughter-in-law kept the hen, so there would be chicks by Christmas. The very same night Malik Tintilinich brought magpie eggs and placed them under the hen to keep as if they were her own.

"Poprskao te kesten iz žeravice," odvraća baka, a Malik Tintilinić u pepelu puca od smijeha.

Kad je snaha otišla da se umije, pokaže baka Maliku Tintiliniću gdje je u komori snaha nasadila kokoš da bude malih pilića za Božić. Još iste noći donese Malik svračjih jaja i podmetne ih pod kokoš umjesto kokošjih.

3.

Zapovjedila snaha baki da dobro pazi na kokoš, pa kad se izlegu pilići, neka joj javi. Pozvat će snaha čitavo selo da vidi kako ona ima pilića za Božić kad ih nitko nema.

Došlo vrijeme, izlegli se svračići. Javi baka snahi da su pilići izašli, a snaha pozove selo. Došle kume i susjede, malo i veliko, a bio tamo i sin bakin. Snaha zapovjedi baki da donese gnijezdo u trijem.

Donese baka gnijezdo, podigoše kokoš, a ono u gnijezdu nešto zakriješti: iskočiše goli svračići, pa skok! skok! po trijemu.

Kada snaha-guja opazila ovako iznenada svračiće, prevari se, polakomi se u njoj zmijina ćud, poletje snaha po trijemu za svračićima i isplazi za nijma svoj tanki i šiljasti jezik kao u šumi.

Vrisnuše i prekrstiše se kume i susjede te povedoše svoju djecu kući, jer upoznaše da je ono zaista šumska guja.

Majka pak radosno pođe do sina govoreći: "Otpremi je, sine, otkud si je doveo, sad si na svoje oči vidio koga u kući hraniš." I mati htjede da ogrli sinka.

Ali sin je bio baš posve budalast čovjek, pa se još više usprkosio i suprot sela i suprot majke i suprot istih svojih očiju: neće da sudi ženi-guji, nego još vikne na majku: "Otkud tebi svračići u to doba, vještice stara? Nosi mi se iz kuće!"

E, sad je mati vidjela da pomoći nema. Zacvili kao ljuta godina i samo umoli da je bar ne tjera iz kuće dok je dan, da ne vidi selo kakvog je sina othranila.

Sin privoli da mati ostane do večera još u kući.

Kad je došla večer, uze baka u torbu nešto kruha i nešto onih luči što joj ih je dalo ubogo djevojče. A onda ode kukajući iz kuće sinove.

Čim je mati prešla preko praga, utrne se vatra na ognjištu i pade raspelo sa stijene. Ostadoše sin i snaha u mračnoj izbi – i sada sin osjeti kako je počinio

The daughter-in-law ordered the old woman to carefully watch the hen and to let her know when the chicks hatched. She would then call the whole village to come and see that she would have chicks for Christmas when no one else would have them.

The time came when the magpie eggs hatched. The old woman told the daughter-in-law that the chicks had arrived, so the daughter-in-law invited the whole village. Godmothers came and the neighbors, the little ones and the big ones, and the old woman's son was there too. The daughter-in-law ordered the old woman to bring the nest by the entrance hall of the house.

The old woman did as she was told and, as they lifted up the hen, there in the nest something shrieked; naked magpies jumped out and hop! hop! hopped to the eaves.

When the daughter-in-law suddenly noticed the magpies, her greedy viper nature overcame her, and she leapt after the magpies on the eaves. Here, just as in the forest, her thin and sharp tongue darted out at them.

The godmothers and the neighbors screamed and crossed themselves. Then they hurriedly took their children home, because they had found out the daughter-in-law was really a forest viper.

The mother proudly went to her son and said: "Take her back where you found her, son. You saw with your own eyes whom you have been feeding in the house." And the mother wanted to embrace her son.

But the son was such a foolish man that he denied the villagers, his mother, and his own eyes. He did not want to judge his viper-wife, and even shouted at his mother: "Where did you get magpies this time of year, you old witch! Go away, and out of my house!"

And now the mother saw that there was no one to help her. She squealed and pleaded only not to be thrown out of the house during the day, so the villagers would not see what kind of son she had brought up.

veliku grehotu na majci, i pokaje se jako. Ali ne smije da ženi o tom govori jer je plašljiv, nego joj kaže: "Hajdemo za materom da vidimo kako će poginuti od studeni."

Skoči veselo zlorada snaha, nađe im kožuhe, obukoše se i odoše izdaleka za staricom.

A baka žalosna ide po snijegu, u po noći, preko polja. Kad je došla na jedno veliko strnište, uhvati je takva studen da nije mogla dalje. Zato izvadi iz torbe one luči, razgrne snijeg i potpali vatru da se malo ugrije.

Jedva se luči rasplamsale, ali ono čudo! Eto iz njih izlaze Domaći, upravo kao da je na kućnom ognjištu!

Iskakuju iz vatre sve uokolo u snijeg, a za njima iskre frcaju na sve strane u tamnu noć.

Milo je baki, gotovo bi proplakala od milinja što je ne ostaviše samu na putu. A oni se kupe oko nje, smiju se i zvižde.

"Božja braćo," reče baka, "nije meni do radosti, nego mi hajde pomozite u nesreći."

Pripovjedi baka Domaćima kako se budalasti sin još više pozlobio na nju otkad se i on i selo uvjerilo da je u snahe zaista gujin jezik.

"Izagnao me, a vi pomozite ako znate."

Malo šute Domaći, malo tepu snijeg s opančića i ne znaju baki savjeta.

Ali onda Malik Tintilinić reče: "Hajdemo do Stribora, starješine našega. On svačemu savjeta znade."

I odmah se Malik popne na glogov grm, zviznu u prste, a ono iz mraka preko tišine dokasa k njima jelen i dvanaest vjeverica.

Posadiše baku na jelena, a Domaći posjedaše na vjeverice i pođoše put šume Striborove.

Jašu oni kroz noć – na jelenu rogovi i paroščići, a na svakom paroščiću zvjezdica. Sjaji se jelen i kazuje put, a za njim juri dvanaest vjeverica, a u svake vjeverice dva oka kao dva draga kamena. Jure oni i žure, a za njima izdaleka trči snaha i sin, sve im nestaje sape.

Tako stigoše do šume Striborove, i ponese jelen baku kroz šumu.

The son agreed that she could stay until night.

At nightfall, the old woman put some bread in a bag and a few of the twigs that the poor girl had given her. She then left the son's house crying.

As soon as the mother crossed the threshold, the fire was extinguished on the hearth and the crucifix fell from the wall. The son and the daughter-in-law remained in the dark hut. Soon the son felt that he had sinned against his mother and felt guilty. But he did not dare say anything about it to his wife because he was afraid, and so he said: "Let's follow mother to see how she freezes to death."

The evil daughter-in-law jumped with joy, got their fur coats, and they began to follow the old woman from afar. The sad old woman walked in the night snow, over the field. When she came to a large field of stubble, she became so cold she could not continue. She pulled the wood chips out of her bag that she had brought, cleared away the snow, and lit a fire to warm herself.

The splinters had just lit when suddenly a miracle happened! Out of them appeared the Domachi, just as they had when she was at home.

They jumped out of the fire and into the snow, and behind them sparks flew all around in the dark night.

The old woman was so pleased that she cried with joy they had not abandoned her, and they gathered around her, laughing and whistling.

"God's brothers," said the old woman, "I am not in the mood for joy, but come and help me in my misfortune."

The old woman told them how her foolish and defiant son had become, once he and the village had seen the daughter-in-law's viper tongue.

"He drove me out, and you help if you know how."

The Domachi were quiet for a while, tapping on the snow with their shoes, because they were not sure what to say to the old woman.

At last Malik Tintilinich said: "Let's go to Stribor, our elder. He has advice for everyone."

Immediately Malik climbed onto the hawthorn tree, whistled with fingers and, out of the darkness in silence, a stag with twelve squirrels came to them.

Spozna snaha sve u mraku da je ovo šuma Striborova gdje je ona već jednom radi grijeha ukleta bila, ali od velike zlobe ne može se ni sjetiti svojih novih grijeha, ni pobojati se za njih, nego se još više raduje govoreći: "Propast će neuka baka u ovoj šumi sred toliko čarolija" i poletje još brže za jelenom.

Donese dakle jelen baku pred Stribora. Stribor pak bijaše šumski starješina. Sjedio je sred šume, u dudu tako velikom da je u njem bilo sedam zlatnih dvorova i osmo selo, srebrnom ogradicom ograđeno. Pred najljepšim dvorom sjedi Stribor na stolici, u crvenoj kabanici.

"Pomozi baki, propala je od snaje-guje," rekoše Domaći Striboru kad mu se bijahu poklonili i oni i baka. Pripovjede oni sve kako je bilo. A snaha i sin došuljali se do duba, pa kroz crvotoč gledaju i slušaju što će biti.

Kad su Domaći svršili svoju pripovijest, reče Stribor baki: "Ne boj se, starice! Ostavi snahu neka živi u zlobi dok je zloba ne dovede opet onamo otkuda se prerano oslobodila. A tebi ću lako pomoći. Gledaj tamo ono selo, srebrom ograđeno!"

Pogleda baka, a ono njezino rodno selo u kojemu je mladovala, a u selu proštenje i veselje. Zvona zvone, gusle gude, zastave se viju, a pjesme podcikuju.

"Uniđi kroz ogradicu, pljesni rukama i pomladit ćeš se odmah. Ostat ćeš u selu svome da mladuješ i da se raduješ, kao pred pedesetak godina!" reče Stribor.

Razveseli se baka kao nikada, poletje odmah do ogradice, uhvatila se već rukom za srebrna vratašca, ali se uto još nečega sjetila, pa upita Stribora: "A što će biti od mog sina?"

"Ne budali, bako!" odgovori Stribor, "otkud bi ti za svoga sina znala? On će ostati u ovom vremenu, a ti ćeš se vratiti u mladost svoju! Ni znati nećeš za kakvog sina!"

Kad je baka ovo čula, zamisli se teško. A onda se polako vrati od ogradice, dođe natrag pred Stribora, nakloni se duboko i reče: "Hvala ti, dobri gospodaru, na svemu dobru što mi ga daješ. Ali ja volim ostati u svojoj nesreći

They helped the old woman mount the stag, and the Domachi sat on the squirrels. They headed towards Stribor's forest.

They rode through the night – on the stag antlers and prongs, and on each prong a little star. The stag shines and shows the path, and behind him run twelve squirrels, and each squirrel with two eyes as two precious stones. They run at full speed and rush; behind them from afar run the daughter-in-law and the son, losing their breath.

Thus they arrived by Stribor's forest and the stag carried the old woman through the forest.

In the darkness the daughter-in-law realized this was Stribor's forest where she once was bewitched because of her sin. But she could not remember her recent sins, and was not afraid, so gleefully she said: "The ignorant old woman will perish in this forest amongst the many spells!" And, even faster she followed behind the stag.

The stag brought the old woman to Stribor. Stribor was the forest's elder chief. He sat in the middle of the forest inside an oak tree so huge that it had room for seven golden palaces in it, as well as a village enclosed by a silver fence. In front of the most beautiful palace sat Stribor on a chair in a red cape.

"Help the old woman who has suffered from her viper daughter-in-law," the Domachi said to Stribor when they and the old woman bowed down before him. They told Stribor everything that had happened. And as they spoke, the daughter-in-law and the son approached the oak tree, and peeked and listened through a wormhole to see what was happening.

When the Domachi finished their story, Stribor said to the old woman: "Don't be afraid, old woman! Let the daughter-in-law live in malice until she again comes to the state from which she was freed too early. And I will easily help you. Look at that village over there with a silver enclosure."

The old woman looked and saw the village where she was born and where she had grown up. In the village there was a church feast going on filled with happiness and joy. The bells were ringing, the gusle was playing, flags were fluttering, and songs were being sung.

a znati da imam sina negoli da mi dadeš sve blago i sve dobro ovoga svijeta a da moram zaboraviti sina!"

Kad je baka ovo izrekla, strahovito jeknu cijela dubrava, prestadoše čari u šumi Striborovoj, jer je baki bila draža njezina nevolja nego sva sreća ovoga svijeta.

Zanjiše se čitava šuma, provali se zemlja, propadne u zemlju ogromni dub sa dvorovima i sa selom srebrom ograđenim, nestade Stribora i Domaćih – ciknu snaha iza duba, pretvori se u guju – uteče u rupu – a majka i sin nađoše se nasred šume sami, jedno uz drugo.

Pade sin pred majku na koljena, ljubi joj skute i rukave, a onda je podiže na svoje ruke i nosi kući kuda sretno do zore stigoše.

Moli sin Boga i majku da mu oproste. Bog mu oprosti, a majka mu nije ni zamjerila bila.

Momak se poslije vjenčao s onim ubogim i milim djevojčetom što im bijaše dovela Domaće u kuću. Još i sad sretno žive svi zajedno, pak im Malik Tintilinić u zimnje večeri rado na ognjište dohodi.

"Enter through the fence, clap your hands, and you will be young again. You will remain in the village to be as young and happy as you were more than fifty years ago!" said Stribor.

The old woman happily ran to the fence, and touched it with her hand, but just then she remembered something and asked Stribor: "And what will become of my son?"

"Don't be silly, old woman!" replied Stribor. "How would you know about your son? He will remain in this time, while you will return to your youth! You will not know of any son!"

When the old woman heard this, she began to think deeply. Then she returned from the fence and came back bowing before him and said: "Thank you, good Master, for everything good that you have given to me. But I want to remain in my misfortune and know that I have a son, rather than receive all the goodness of this world and have to forget him!"

When the old woman said this, the whole forest resounded and the spells ceased in Stribor's forest, because the old woman would rather keep her misfortune than have all the happiness of this world.

The whole forest rocked, the earth fell in, and the huge oak and its palaces and silver fenced village sank underground. Stribor and all the Domachi also vanished; the daughter-in-law shrieked from behind the oak, turned back into a viper, and wriggled into a hole. Within moments, mother and son found each other side by side in the middle of the forest.

The son fell on his knees before his mother, kissed the hem of her dress and the sleeves, then lifted her up in his arms and carried her home where they arrived at dawn.

The son prayed God and his mother to forgive him. God forgave him, and his mother wasn't angry with him.

Later, the young man married the poor peasant young girl who had brought the Domachi to their home. They live happily even now, all together, and during winter nights Malik Tintilinich joyfully visits their hearth.

Unborn Maiden

Nerođena Djevojka

NEROĐENA DJEVOJKA

*N*eki je carević načinio bunar usred svoga dvorca. Iz bunara su tekli med i mlijeko. Stadoše dolaziti djevojke iz cijeloga carstva da sebi natoče meda i mlijeka. Carević ih promatraše iz dvorca. Htio je izabrati najljepšu djevojku i njom se oženiti.

Jednoć dođe na bunar zgrbljena bakica. Napuni sebi vrčeve. Počne nalijevati med i mlijeko u ljuske jajeta. Carević baci kamen i razbije ljuske. Baka ga pogleda. Reče mu: "Dao Gospod, sinko, da se oženiš nerođenom djevojkom!"

"Gdje ću je naći, bako?" zapita carević.

"Ne znam," odvrati baka i ode.

Prođe mnogo vremena. Carević se nije mogao oženiti. Nije mu se svidjela ni jedna od djevojaka koje su dolazile na bunar.

Jednog dana reče carević svojoj majci: "To je razumljivo, majko, kad se moram oženiti nerođenom djevojkom, kako mi je kazala ona bakica. Ali gdje da nađem takvu djevojku?"

"Zapitaj Sunce, sinko," odvrati mu majka. "Ono svijetli svisoka i vidi naširoko, ono će znati gdje je nerođena djevojka."

Carević krene da nađe Sunce. Hodao je, hodao, prošao mnoga polja, mnoge rijeke i planine. Ali Sunčevih dvoraca nigdje ne ugleda. Uspne se na visoku planinu. Naiđe na starog ovčara. Reče mu: "Dobar dan, djede. Znaš li gdje stanuje Sunce?"

"Što će ti Sunce, sinko?"

"Želim ga zapitati gdje ću naći nerođenu djevojku, pa da se oženim njome."

Starac pokaže rukom prema zapadu i reče: "Vidiš li one tri planine, što

UNBORN MAIDEN

*T*here once was a prince who dug a well in the middle of his palace. From the well flowed milk and honey. Maidens from the whole kingdom began to come to the well to pour themselves some milk and honey. The prince watched them from the palace. He wanted to choose the prettiest one to marry.

One day an old hunchbacked woman came to the well. She filled her jugs, then began to pour milk and honey into egg shells. The prince threw a stone that broke the shells. The old woman looked at him and said: "Let it be God's will, son, that you marry an unborn maiden!"

"Where will I find her, old woman?" asked the prince.

"I don't know," replied the old woman as she left.

Much time passed and the prince did not marry. He did not like a single maiden who came to the well. One day the prince said to his mother: "It seems, Mother, that I'll have to marry an unborn maiden, as the old woman said. But where will I find such a maiden?"

"Ask the Sun, my child. It shines from high above and sees the whole wide world. It will know where the unborn maiden is."

The prince set out to find the Sun. He walked and walked, passing many fields, many rivers and mountains. But he did not see any Sun palaces. He climbed up a high mountain, saw an old shepherd and said to him: "Good day, grandfather. Do you know where the Sun lives?"

"Why do you need to know, my son?"

"I wish to ask the Sun where the unborn maiden lives, so that I can marry her."

The old man pointed his hand towards the West and said: "Do you see those three mountains that lie next to each other? If you pass all three, you

se nižu jedna iza druge? Pošto ih priječeš sve tri, naći ćeš se pred velikim zlatnim vratima, a iza njih je prekrasni vrt. Tamo stanuje Sunce. Čekaj dok se na planinama smrači, i čim se zasvijetli u vrtu, pokucaj na vrata."

Carević opet krene. Hodao je, hodao, prešao prvu planinu, prešao drugu, prevalio i treću.

Stigao do čarobnog vrta ograđenog bijelim kamenom, a u ogradi zlatna vrata. Uskoro se naokolo smrači, a u vrtu bljesnuše prozori na Sunčevim dvorima.

Carević pokuca na vrata.

Iziđe Sunčeva majka. Zapita ga: "Što tražiš, momče?"

"Dođoh da mi Sunce kaže gdje ću naći nerođenu djevojku da se oženim njome."

Sunčeva majka odvrati: "Sunce je sad umorno i srdito. Ali ja ću ti kazati kako ćeš naći ono za čim si pošao u potragu."

Sunčeva majka otkine tri jabuke i reče: "Uzmi, momče, ove jabuke. Kad dođeš do vode, razreži jednu. Iz nje će izići lijepa djevojka. Čim ona tebi kaže: "Daj mi, brate, vodice," ti joj daj i ona će ostati s tobom."

Carević uzme jabuke. Krene.

Hodao je, hodao – ne naiđe na vodu, ožedni.

Razreže jednu jabuku da okvasi usta.

Iz jabuke iziđe lijepa djevojka i reče: "Daj mi, brate, vodice!"

"Nemam je," odvrati carević. Djevojka nestane.

Carević krene dalje. Opet ožedni. Razreže drugu jabuku. Iz nje iziđe još ljepša djevojka i reče: "Daj mi, brate, vodice!"

"Nemam," odvrati carević.

I ta djevojka nestane.

Carević opet krene dalje. Hodao je, hodao – stigao do nekog bunara. Razrezao i treću jabuku. Iz nje čarobna ljepotica, blještava kao Sunce. I ona reče: "Brate, daj mi vodice!"

Carević joj da, i ona ostane s njim.

"Hoćeš li se udati za me?" zapita je on.

will find yourself in front of a large golden gate, and behind it is a beautiful garden. There lives the Sun. Wait until the mountains are dark and, as soon as there is light in the garden, knock at the door."

The prince started out again. He walked and walked, passing the first mountain, the second, and the third. He came to the enchanted garden enclosed by a white stone fence. He saw a golden door in the fence. Soon it got dark all around and in the garden the windows began to shine on the Sun's palaces.

The prince knocked on the door and the Sun's mother appeared and asked: "What are you looking for, young man?"

"I came to ask the Sun to tell me where I can find the unborn maiden, so I can marry her."

The Sun's mother replied: "The Sun is now tired and angry. But I will tell you how to find what you are looking for."

The Sun's mother picked three apples and said: "Take the apples, young man. When you come to water, cut one. From it will appear a beautiful maiden. As soon as she tells you, 'Give me, brother, water,' give it to her, and she will remain with you."

The prince took the apples and set out.

He walked and walked. He didn't find any water and grew thirsty, so he cut one apple to wet his dry mouth. A beautiful maiden appeared from the apple and said: "Give me, brother, water!"

"I don't have any," the prince replied.

The maiden instantly disappeared.

The prince went on farther and again he became thirsty, so he cut another apple. From it appeared an even more beautiful maiden who said: "Give me, brother, water!"

"I don't have any," the prince responded again.

And that maiden, too, disappeared.

The prince continued his search. He walked and walked and arrived at a well where he cut the third apple, and from it appeared a miraculous beauty, bright as the Sun. And she said: "Brother, give me some water!"

"Hoću," odvrati djevojka.

"Znaš li kamo ću te odvesti?"

"Ne znam."

"U carski dvorac. Počekaj malo na onoj vrbi. Doći ću po tebe s carskim kolima. Dovest ću svirače i svatove kao što je običaj."

Carević posjedne djevojku na vrbu kraj bunara i ode.

Ne prođe mnogo vremena, na bunar dođe neka Ciganka. Ugleda djevojku. Zapita je: "Koga tu čekaš, djevojko?"

"Carevića," odvrati djevojka. "Doći će po mene sa sviračima i svatovima."

"Tako? Samo da uzmem vode, pa da se maknem odavde. Neću da me zateknu carski svatovi. Oh, kako li je teško izvući vodu iz ovog bunara! Ne mogu izvući vedro!"

"Vuci, vuci … izvadit ćeš ga," reče ljepotica.

"Ne mogu, sestrice."

"Počekaj da siđem da ti pomognem."

Djevojka siđe. Izvuče vodu. Ciganka napuni sebi vrč i reče: "Znaš li što, sestrice? Obuci moje haljine, a ja ću tvoje. Ogledat ćemo se u bunaru da vidimo koja je ljepša: ti ili ja."

Zamijeniše haljine. Ogledajući se Ciganka gurne nerođenu djevojku u bunar i uspne se na vrbu. Dođoše svatovi. Carević pogleda gore na vrbu. Ne prepozna djevojke.

"Što si tako pocrnjela, djevojko?" zapita.

"Od sunca," odgovori Ciganka.

Odjenuše mladu u svadbenu haljinu. Odvedu je u carski dvorac. Prirediše svadbu.

Prođe neko vrijeme, carević jednoć ode da napoji svoga konja na bunaru gdje je po prvi put ugledao nerođenu djevojku. Ali konj se uzjoguni. Nije se htio približiti vodi … Carević zapovjedi neka isprazne bunar. Htjede vidjeti čega se plaši njegov konj. Izvukavši svu vodu, u bunaru nađoše zlatnu ribicu.

The prince gave it to her and she remained with him.

"Will you marry me?" he asked the maiden.

"I will," the maiden replied.

"Do you know where I will take you?"

"I don't know."

"To the king's palace. Wait for a while on that willow. I will come back with the king's carriage to pick you up. I will bring musicians and a wedding party as is our custom."

The prince put the maiden on the willow by the well and left. Soon after, a Gypsy girl came up to the well, saw the maiden and asked her: "For whom are you waiting, young woman?"

"The prince," the girl answered. "He will come back for me with musicians and a wedding party."

"Is that so? Let me just take the water and I will go from here. I don't want to be here for the prince's wedding. Oh, how hard it is to pull up the water from this well! I cannot pull up the pail."

"Pull! Pull! You'll get it up!" said the beauty.

"I can't, sister."

"Wait, I'll get down to help you."

The young woman made her way down and helped pull up the water. The Gypsy filled her jug and said: "You know what, sister? Put on my dress, and I'll put on yours. We'll look at ourselves in the well and see who is prettier, you or I."

They exchanged dresses. While looking at themselves, the Gypsy pushed the unborn maiden into the well and climbed up the willow. The wedding party arrived. The prince looked up at the willow and didn't recognize the girl.

"Why are you so dark, maiden?" he asked.

"From the sun," replied the Gypsy.

They dressed her in the wedding dress and took her to the king's castle. They prepared the wedding.

Some time passed and one day the prince went to water his horse at the

Priediše ribicu i carević je pojede. Kad su bacili kosti, jedna kost padne u vrt ispod carevićevog prozora. Iz te je kosti izrasla visoka topola. Dosegla je čak do prozora. Čim bi se pokazala carica, topola bi je šibala svojim tankim granama. A kad bi se pojavio carević, topola bi ga milovala.

Ciganka zapovjedi neka posijeku topolu. Kad su je sjekli, dođe neka bakica i sakupi trijeske. Odnese ih kući. Jedna joj se treščica svidjela. Ona je digne na policu.

Kad bi baka nekamo otišla, treščica bi se pretvorila u djevojku. Ona bi mela i spremala. Onda bi se opet pretvorila u trijesku. Baka bi se, vrativši se, čudom čudila tko joj sprema kuću.

Često je govorila: "Ej, ti što mi rediš! Pokaži se! Ako si momak, bit ćeš mi sin! Ako si djevojka, bit ćeš mi kći!"

Djevojka je sve čula, ali je šutjela.

Jedno jutro baka se sakrije iza vrata.

Tek što je djevojka sišla s police, baka radosno klikne: "Stoj djevojko! Bit ćeš mi kći!"

I baka i djevojka stale živjeti kao majka i kći.

Jadanput se dogodi da je carica pokidala svoju ogrlicu. Pozvaše sve djevojke iz castva, ali ni jedna nije mogla nanizati biserna zrnca ogrlice kako treba.

Dođe red na bakinu djevojku. Ona sjedne na carski divan. Oko nje se sakupili car i svi dvorjani. Koliko god je bakina djevojka bila lijepa, postane još ljepša kad je ušla u carski dvorac. Svi su bili očarani njenom ljepotom. Nisu skidali očiju s nje.

I ona počne nizati bisere. Nizala je i redajući govorila: "Živio jednoć neki carević. Sagradio je čudnovati bunar. Iz njega su tekli med i mlijeko…"

Tako je djevojka, bez prekida, ispripovijedala sve što se zbilo. Stigavši do onoga kako ju je Ciganka gurnula u bunar, carević skoči. Zagrli bakinu djevojku i reče:"Razumio sam, sve sam razumio! Ti ćeš mi biti žena!"

On se oženi lijepom djevojkom, a Ciganku protjera kroz devet sela u deseto.

well where he had seen the maiden for the first time. But the horse was fearful and didn't want to approach the well. The prince ordered that the well be emptied so that he could find out why his horse was so afraid. Once they took all the water out, they found a little golden fish.

They prepared the fish and the prince ate it. When they took away the bones, one bone fell in the yard under the prince's window. Out of this bone grew a tall poplar tree. It reached up to the window. As soon as the Gypsy-princess appeared, the poplar would whip her with its thin branches. And when the prince showed up, the poplar would caress him.

The Gypsy ordered that they cut down the poplar tree. While they were cutting it, an old woman appeared, picked up the fallen wooden chips, and took them home. She thought one of the chips was pretty and put it on a shelf.

When the old woman would go somewhere, the wood fragment would transform into a maiden. She would sweep and put everything in order and turn back again into a piece of wood. Upon her return, the old woman would wonder who had cleaned her house. She often said: "Hey, you who clean my house! Show yourself! If you are a young man, you'll be my son! If you are a maiden, you'll be my daughter!"

The girl heard everything but kept quiet, so one morning the old woman hid behind the door.

As soon as the girl came down from the shelf, the old woman happily shouted: "Stop, maiden! You'll be my daughter!" The old woman and the girl began to live as mother and daughter.

Once, it happened that the queen's precious necklace broke. Although all maidens were summoned in the kingdom, not one of them could thread the diamonds on the necklace correctly. Then came the old woman's daughter turn. She sat on the king's sofa. Around her gathered the king and all the members of the castle. As much as the old woman's daughter was beautiful, she became even more beautiful when she entered the king's palace. All were enchanted by her beauty. They could not take their eyes off her.

And she began to thread the diamonds. She threaded them while telling this story:

"Once there lived a prince. He built a miraculous well. From it flowed milk and honey…"

Thus, the maiden without stopping recounted everything that had transpired. When she reached the part about the Gypsy pushing her into the well, the prince jumped up, embraced the old woman's daughter and said: "I understand, I understand everything! You will be my wife!"

He married the beautiful maiden, and the Gypsy was banished beyond the ninth village into the tenth one.

APPENDIX

DODATAK

GLOSSARY

Bura – Old North-eastern wind, tempest.

Dazhbog – Son of Svarog, linked with fire.

Domachi/Domovoy – Slavic house spirits, who live in the hearth, spoil things or do good. The root *dom* means house, home.

Gusle – One-stringed folk fiddle.

Jugo – South wind, souther.

Khors – Slavic deity linked with the Moon, light (winter sun).

Kolede – Winter celebration which takes place at the end of December in honor of the Sun, marking those days when it again appears.

Mok, Mokosh/Makosh – A powerful force in marshes, linked with the Earth and an aid to Perun. Mother Earth, goddess of fertility, moisture.

Nijemi jezik – Ancient Slavs believed that animals speak a special language and that some people are able to understand it.

Otok Bujan – An island overflowing with vegetation. Ancient Slavic image of heaven.

Perun – Chief god of war, god of thunder and lightning (resides in oak trees).

Simargl – Slavic deity linked with fire and hearth.

Stribog, Stribor – Atmospheric deity, linked with wind and storm.

Svarog – God-Creator, solar deity, god of the skies and fire.

Svarozhich – Son of Svarog, sunlight on earth.

Veles, Volos, Vlas – Chthonic deity, protector of livestock and wealth, opponent of Perun.

SLAVIC MYTHOLOGICAL NAMES

SVAROG
Fire

SOLAR (Sun, Sky)

PERUN — Chief God of War/Thunder

VELES — Chthonic Deity, Livestock, Wealth

ATMOSPHERIC (Air)

STRIBOG
(Wind/Storm)

DAZHBOG
Son of Svarog
(Fire)

KHORS
(Moon, Thunder,
Light, Winter Sun)

EARTH

MOKOSH-EARTH GODDESS
(Moist Mother Earth)

SIMARGL
(Crops, Vegetation)

WATER

BIBLIOGRAPHY

Hrvatske bajke i basne. Introduced by Ivica Matičević. Zagreb: Alfa, 1997.

Hrvatske narodne bajke. Edited by Ranka Javor. Zagreb: Mozaik knjiga, 2008.

Hrvatske narodne pripovijetke. Edited by Dr. Hrvojka Mihanović. Zagreb: Znanje, 2006.

Hrvatskih narodnih pripovijedaka. Collected by Rudolf Strohal. Book I, volume II. *Narodne pripovijetke iz sela Stativa*, 4th ed. Zagreb: Knjižara St. Kugli, n.d. 1912.

Ilustrirane hrvatske bajke. Selected and Edited by Ranka Javor. Zagreb: ABC, 1997.

I. Brlić-Mažuranić, A. Milćinović, Z. Marković. *Izabrana djela*. Edited by Miroslav Šicel. Pet stoljeća hrvatske književnosti. Book 73. Zagreb: Matica hrvatska, Zora, 1968.

"Introduction: The Folktale." *An Anthology of Russian Folktales*. Translated and Edited by Jack V. Haney. Armonk, N.Y.: M. E. Sharpe, 2009.

Ivana Brlić-Mažuranić. *Priče iz davnine*. Prepared by Sanja Božić. Zagreb: Školska knjiga, 2007.

Ivana Brlić-Mažuranić. *Priče iz davnine*. Zagreb: Mladost, 1975.

Izabrane narodne pripovijetke. Edited by Dr. David Bogdanović. Zagreb: Kr. Hrv.-Slov.-Dalm. zem. vlade., 1914.

Narodne pripovijetke. Edited by Dr. Branko Magarašević. Zageb: Prosvjeta, 1951.

Narodne pripovijetke. Edited by Maja Bošković-Stulli. Pet stoljeća hrvatske književnosti, Book 26. Zagreb: Matica hrvatska, Zora, 1963.

Warner, Marina. *Once Upon a Time: A Short History of Fairy Tale*. Oxford: Oxford University Press, 2014.

BIOGRAPHIES

Josip Botteri Dini, a well-known Croatian artist, was born in Zagreb and grew up in Split on the Dalmatian coast. He first attended high school in Zagreb at a seminary, an experience that left a significant and fruitful impact on the life of the artist. In early childhood he was also influenced by his uncle Josip Botteri, who was an artist and who helped him decide on selecting the Art Academy for his future. In Split he graduated from high school in 1963 and the following year was accepted to the Academy in Zagreb, completing his studies in 1968. Various contemporary exhibits influenced his work, such as exhibits by Pablo Picasso and Victor Vasarely, whose use of color certainly attracted the young Botteri.

After the Academy he returned again to the Dalmatian coast and opened in Split *Salon d'Art*. He held his first solo exhibit in Split in 1970. In addition he taught classes at various schools and traveled abroad. At an exhibit in Milano he received his first award in 1973. In 1975 he stopped teaching to devote his life exclusively to art.

In the following decades, Mr. Botteri held exhibits in main galleries throughout Croatia and traveled abroad to Italy, France, Spain and the United States. He taught at the Academy of Fine Arts in Split and was director of the Art Gallery in Split, as well as in Bol on the island of Brač. We find his works in permanent collections in Milano, Paris, Chicago, and throughout Croatia. In his work he employs different techniques, using oil, acrylic, serigraph, stained glass, and mosaic. He has done numberless works for monasteries, as well as mosaics and stained windows for churches in Croatia, Italy, Austria and Australia. In 1995 and 2016 he received his most significant awards for contributions to cultural life. He lives and works in Split, Croatia.

Dasha C. Nisula completed her Doctorate in Comparative Literature at the University of Southern California. She began teaching at USC, then at Baylor University, and at Western Michigan University, where she is Professor Emeritus and Faculty Fellow of Lee Honors College. For most of her career she has been teaching Russian and Croatian languages, literature, and culture, as well as translating poetry and short stories from these languages. She is author of six books, numerous articles, reviews, and translations which have appeared in books as *An Anthology of South Slavic Literatures* and *Duet of Iron*, as well as in literary journals as *Modern Poetry in Translation*, *Southwestern Review*, *International Poetry Review*, *Massachusetts Review* and *American Journal of Ophthalmology* among others. A member of the American Literary Translators Association, she lives and works in Kalamazoo, Michigan.

ACKNOWLEDGEMENTS

I want to thank Ms. Elizabeth Marquart for reading and offering comments on the first drafts of these fairy tales. And my thanks go to Dr. Roxanne Panicacci for her final reading of the manuscript. I am grateful to the Croatian artist Mr. Josip Botteri Dini who graciously agreed to illustrate these fairy tales and prepare the cover for the book. In order to complete this project, I am indebted to Ms. Julie Hayward of Western Michigan University libraries for her knowledge and help in finding various sources. Last but not least, I wish to thank Mr. Michael Callaghan, Publisher of Exile Editions, for his interest in this work, and for providing me with the opportunity to build a body of translations, including *You With Hands More Innocent* by Vesna Parun, *Music is Everything* by Slavko Mihalić, and the forthcoming anthology, *Rhythm and Free Verse Across the Slavic Belt*.

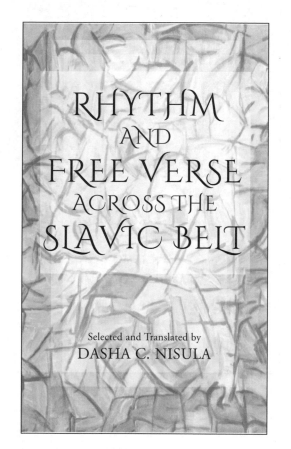

RHYTHM
AND
FREE VERSE
ACROSS THE
SLAVIC BELT

Selected and Translated by
DASHA C. NISULA

Selected by translator Dasha C. Nisula, this unique volume traces the development of modern free verse that extends from Croatia on the Adriatic to Russia in the East.

Included are early pieces from the West to East Slavic belt, with the majority of the works focusing on the Russian Whitmanist Vladimir Burich, and the contemporary master of free verse in Russia, Vyacheslav Kupriyanov. This volume captures feeling, essence, rhythm, and depth through superb translations.

Includes an Introduction by the translator, and endworks: "Vladimir Burich Unbound" with Notes, "Reflections on Free Verse" by Arvo Mets, a Vladimir Burich bibliography, a Vyacheslav Kupriyanov bibliography with Awards, an alphabetical listing About the Poets (West Slavic Belt and East Slavic Belt), and a Translator's Note.

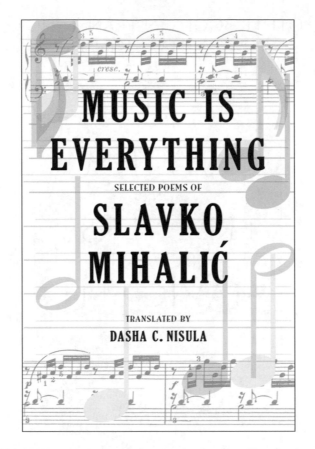

MUSIC IS EVERYTHING

SELECTED POEMS OF

SLAVKO MIHALIĆ

TRANSLATED BY

DASHA C. NISULA

Slavko Mihalić (1928-2007), upon finishing high school, moved to Zagreb where he worked for a newspaper and published his first book of poetry, *Komorna muzika* (*Chamber Music*) in 1954. During the course of his life, he worked as an anthologist, publisher, editor, critic, writer for children, authored over twenty books of poetry, and established several literary journals and the literary review *Most* (*Bridge*), which brought Croatian literature to international readers. Translated into major world languages, Slavko Mihalić is a recipient of numerous literary awards, among them Tin Ujević, City of Zagreb, Matica Hrvatska, Miroslav Krleža, Goranov Vjenac, Vladimir Nazor and others.

Early on in his life Slavko Mihalić also became a musician. Bach and Mozart inspired him and the musicality of these masters he applied to the word. And through the word in this volume one can detect the wondrous nature of this artist. The poems in this edition are taken from his last three publications: *Sabrane pjesme* (*Collected Poems*), 1998; *Akordeon* (*Accordion*), 2000; and *Močvara* (*Marsh*), 2004.

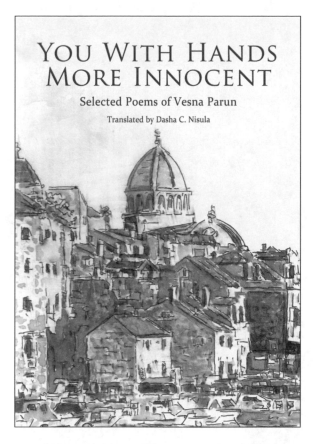

YOU WITH HANDS
MORE INNOCENT

Selected Poems of Vesna Parun

Translated by Dasha C. Nisula

Vesna Parun was born in 1922 on the island of Zlarin, on the Dalmatian coast of Croatia. She made her literary debut in 1947 with the collection of poems, *Zore i vihori (Dawns and Hurricanes)*, and over the next 60 years went on to publish more than twenty books of poetry, as well as essays, criticism, and children's books. Although Croatian lyrical is a strong and fruitful tradition, until Vesna Parun there was not a single female poet with such developed sensibilities and poetic expressiveness: Parun's *modus vivendi* was "it is love that makes and keeps us human." And while there are many poets in Croatian literature who have written collections of love poetry, about love of a woman as an object, here we have poems about love with a woman as subject.

The poems in this edition are deeply moving, and great examples of language that exposes Eastern European culture to the English-speaking world – a volume that captures the feeling, essence, rhythm, and depth of the author's words as best as English can through superb translations.

WITH ILLUSTRATIONS BY MARKO MARIAN